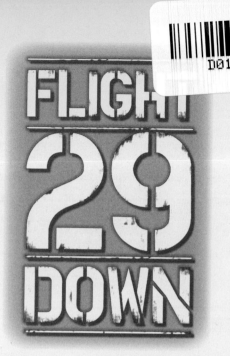

The Seven

Stan Rogow Productions · Grosset & Dunlap

GROSSET & DUNLAP
Published by the Penguin Group
Penguin Group (USA) Inc., 375 Hudson Street, New York, New York 10014, U.S.A.
Penguin Group (Canada), 90 Eglinton Avenue East, Suite 700, Toronto, Ontario, Canada M4P 2Y3
(a division of Pearson Penguin Canada Inc.)
Penguin Books Ltd, 80 Strand, London WC2R 0RL, England
Penguin Ireland, 25 St Stephen's Green, Dublin 2, Ireland
(a division of Penguin Books Ltd)
Penguin Group (Australia), 250 Camberwell Road, Camberwell, Victoria 3124, Australia
(a division of Pearson Australia Group Pty Ltd)
Penguin Books India Pvt Ltd, 11 Community Centre, Panchsheel Park, New Delhi - 110 017, India
Penguin Group (NZ), Cnr Airborne and Rosedale Roads, Albany, Auckland 1310, New Zealand
(a division of Pearson New Zealand Ltd)
Penguin Books (South Africa) (Pty) Ltd, 24 Sturdee Avenue, Rosebank, Johannesburg 2196, South Africa

Penguin Books Ltd, Registered Offices:
80 Strand, London WC2R 0RL, England

Published by Grosset & Dunlap, a division of Penguin Young Readers Group, 345 Hudson Street, New York, New York 10014. GROSSET & DUNLAP is a trademark of Penguin Group (USA) Inc. Printed in the U.S.A.

Library of Congress Cataloging-in-Publication Data

Vornholt, John.
The seven : a novelization / by John Vornholt.
p. cm. — (Flight 29 Down ; #2)
"Adapted from the teleplays by D.J. MacHale."
"Based on the TV series created by D.J. MacHale."
ISBN 0-448-44107-1
I. MacHale, D. J. II. Title. III. Series.
PZ7.V946Sev 2006
2005027529

10 9 8 7 6 5 4 3 2 1

FLIGHT 29 DOWN

The Seven

A novelization by
John Vornholt
Adapted from the
teleplays by D.J. MacHale

Based o **TV series created by**
D.J. MacHale
Stan Rogow

Stan Rogow Productions · Grosset & Dunlap

**Many thanks to Walter Sorrells,
for his helpful insight on
this book and this series.**

PROLOGUE

There was a huge, sickening bang from the rear of the plane. Flames were streaming from the engines on the right. Someone was screaming.

Jackson rushed to the front of the plane. "What's happening?" he shouted, jerking back the curtain that separated him and his fellow passengers from the cockpit.

Only, there was no pilot in the cockpit. Terror hit him like a hammer.

Where had the pilot gone? Flames were licking at the instrument panel. Through the windshield Jackson could see nothing but ocean. The airplane seemed to be flying straight down on a crash course with the water. How high were they? Probably not even high enough to pull up before they slammed into the water.

He threw himself into the pilot's seat. How did this thing work? He'd played Flight Simulator—so he ought to be able to figure it out, right? There was a yoke that was sort of like a steering wheel. Maybe if he pulled back on it.

He pulled, straining to take control. But the yoke was stuck.

Jackson could hear all the kids in the back of the plane—all the kids from the Hartwell School who were with him on the eco-camping tour to the Pacific island of Palau—screaming in terror. The shrieks of fear joined with the howling of wind as the terrible storm pounded the laboring aircraft.

Why wouldn't the steering mechanism move?

Jackson hauled on the stick with all his might. He could see the waves rising up out of the ocean now—massive, white-capped waves, big enough to swallow an ocean liner.

They were all going to die.

Jackson was sure of it. He kept pulling and pulling on the yoke, trying to get the nose of the plane up, but it was hopeless. He felt a wave of regret and anger. Why had the pilot disappeared? Why had he abandoned them? This was all *wrong*!

The plane spun and spun, and Jackson pulled and pulled. He could feel every muscle straining. Sweat poured out of him.

They were all going to die.

The noise of the airplane had become deafening—a heavy, slow thudding noise that seemed to signal imminent death. And permeating everything was a powerful smell. It was weird, but it smelled like—

"Nooooooo!" he screamed.

The smell grew stronger as the waves grew closer. The smell of—

"Noooooooooo!"

It was all up to him, and he was failing them. Failing himself and failing them all. No matter how hard he pulled, it wasn't hard enough, and the smell was getting stronger and stronger.

"Noooooooooo!"

The waves rose closer and closer and closer and everybody was going to die and the flames were pouring out of the instrument panel and the plane was spinning and bucking and the kids were screaming and every muscle in his body was straining to pull back the yoke, pull back the yoke, pull back the yoke, and it wouldn't budge and they were all going to die if he didn't do something and everything smelled like . . .

Mac and cheese?

ONE

"**D**ude!"

Jackson blinked, looked around.

Mac and cheese. Mac and cheese. Was he going crazy? The smell was still there. Which was impossible.

The scene looked like a brochure from a travel agency. Lazy turquoise surf lapping at the white sand, endless blue ocean, and steamy breezes tickling the palm trees. Exotic birds hooted in the jungle. And hanging over it all—the heavy scent of salt and flowers that smelled like cheap aftershave. But somewhere beneath it was another smell. Macaroni and cheese? Was that possible?

"Dude!" It was that irritating little guy, Eric, his straw hat tipped back on his head, leaning over Jackson. "Dude, I think you were having a bad dream."

Jackson stood up, brushed the sand off his pants. He was soaked with sweat, and he still felt panicky from the dream.

Looking around at all this island paradise scenery, it was easy to forget just how desperate their situation was.

"You were like all *'RRRRRRrrrrrrr! Uhhnnhhh!'* " Eric said, screwing up his face and making this weird, grating noise. "And you were pulling on your own leg. *RRRRRrrrrrr! Uhhhhnnnhh! RRRRRrrrr!* You were cracking me up! It was pretty doofy-looking."

Jackson gave Eric his coldest gaze.

Eric backed up nervously. "I don't mean like doofy in a bad way. I just mean . . ." He cleared his throat nervously. "Yeah. So. Okay, I'll just be kinda . . ."—he started walking away—". . . moving along."

Macaroni and cheese. Jackson sniffed the air. Swear to God, he could smell it. Behind all the salt air and the exotic aftershave-smelling plants, there it was. Mac and cheese. Was he still dreaming? Jackson had never been the biggest fan of mac and cheese. But right now he'd about kill for it.

Too bad they couldn't eat the flowers or the sand, because they had plenty of both. This South Seas paradise looked terrific, but there was just one thing missing . . .

Food.

He could still remember the picture in the brochure for this fancy field trip that he and the other kids were on. It showed all these happy, grinning kids sitting around a campfire drinking sodas, their plates piled with great-looking food that had just been cooked over an open flame. The brochure had kinda left out a few crucial bits, though. For instance: the storm that smashed up their plane, forcing it to crash-land on this isolated little island. That storm had made a few changes in their itinerary. *Like we don't know where we are, or how long we're going to be stuck here.*

It was the third day after the crash of charter plane 29 DWN on this crummy uninhabited island somewhere in the

South Pacific. At least they *thought* it was uninhabited—although they hadn't explored very much of it. That job was up to their pilot, a sweaty bald guy named Captain Robert Russell, and the three students who had marched off with him. Jory, Ian, and Abby. Weren't those their names?

Maybe I should have gone with them, thought Jackson, *instead of babysitting this car pool of spoiled brats. But Captain Russell and the others have been gone for three days. If there's a resort hotel just beyond the treetops, they should have found it by now.*

Seven of us left. And everyone's big solution to survival is to elect me *leader?* Okay, it isn't their fault. They had to elect somebody, and they're competing against one another. They probably figured he was the unknown quantity, so they might as well dump the thankless job on him. The perfect one to lead them blindly into the unknown.

Which probably explained Jackson's dream. The lives of seven kids felt like way too much responsibility for a fifteen-year-old kid. It was his subconscious telling him . . . well, who really cared what his subconscious was telling him? If he couldn't find some food for the group pretty soon, they'd all starve to death.

Most of the survivors were sitting on the sand around the wrecked DeHavilland Heron airplane. Jackson remembered how they had fought the tide to save the battered plane on that first wild day. They always came back to the hulk, even though it was useless except for storage. Somehow it made them feel a little closer to civilization, a little less cut off, a little less abandoned in the wilderness.

The only one who was missing from the group sitting around the plane was Daley Marin. She must have been off somewhere, overachieving as usual. The do-gooder, Melissa

Wu, stared at Jackson. He hoped she didn't expect him to *do* something, because he was out of ideas. She was always looking at him with wide eyes like she was waiting for him to come up with some big solution to all of life's problems.

You elected me island chief, but you didn't give me the manual.

He liked Daley's little brother, Lex, who was sort of a whiz-kid. The others were a mixed bag. Nathan McHugh was a hard worker and was acting pretty cool about losing the election for leader, but he was one of those leap-before-you-look guys, always getting in hot water because he jumped into something half-cocked.

The other two . . . they seemed pretty useless. One of them was this blond girl, Taylor Hagan. She was a honey, but selfish, spoiled, and dumb as a bag of rocks. The other was the class clown, Eric McGorrill. He and Taylor both seemed to be in a little world by themselves, totally out of touch with just how bad their situation was.

At least the survivors had fresh water now. Daley had discovered a well. But their food was close to running out.

Melissa looked away from Jackson and shrugged her shoulders. "Okay, I'll say it. We're gonna be here for a while, aren't we?"

She was brave, just coming out with that, Jackson thought. Although everyone was thinking it, except for Taylor, who didn't do much thinking. The pretty blonde started to argue the point, but then just shook her head and looked down.

Jackson sniffed the air. There it was again. Mac and cheese. It couldn't be, though, could it? His stomach grumbled. They'd been on half-rations for a day now and he was starving.

"There hasn't been a single search plane," Lex said,

taking off his baseball hat and gazing at the cloud-dappled sky.

"They'll find us," Nathan answered, sounding too confident. He cleared his throat and added, "Eventually."

Eric gave a hollow laugh. "That's what my father said when I asked if he was gonna take me to a Lakers game. He said 'eventually.' "

"How long did it take?" Melissa asked, trying to sound upbeat.

Eric shrugged. "I gave up asking . . . eventually."

"What about that pilot person?" Taylor asked with a pout. "He could still find help. Right?"

"Yeah, eventually," Eric answered. "Which means 'never,' for those of you not keeping up."

Yep, the denial phase is definitely over, Jackson thought. *We're all in agreement on one thing . . . we're in a mess.*

Nathan broke the silence. "Can we talk about something less depressing?"

"Okay. I'm starving," Eric said.

Melissa peered at him and asked, "That's not depressing?"

"Best I could do," he answered.

Grinning cheerfully, Daley walked up to them carrying a makeshift tray of little cups. "Dinner is served!" she announced.

All of them cheered and sat up in attention on the wing of the plane. "Mac and cheese. Food of the gods," she added. "Two hundred and fifty yummy calories made just the way Mom used to . . . straight from a package."

So that was it! Jackson wasn't crazy after all. He really *had* smelled the stuff.

"I hate mac and cheese," Eric said with a frown. "Gimme." He hungrily grabbed a cup and dug in with his fingers.

Daley offered a cup to Taylor, who wrinkled her pretty nose and said, "No, thanks. I'm watching my carbs."

"Yeah, me too!" Daley gave Taylor a broad, bogus smile. Then the smile went away. "I'm gonna watch them go into your face. Eat!"

Taylor blinked like she was afraid Daley might actually pound her in the face. She took a cup of the bright yellow noodles, then looked around and frowned. "Eat with my fingers?"

"Yeah, sorry, the fine silverware was on the other plane," Daley muttered. She took the last cup and sat on the wing with the rest of them.

"Hey, I'll eat yours if you don't want it," Eric said, reaching toward Taylor.

Taylor snatched the cup of macaroni away from Eric.

Everybody dug in with their fingers and wolfed the noodles down. Then they turned the little cups inside out to suck them dry, and licked their fingers until every last scrap of food was gone. Taylor kept looking around expectantly, like she was waiting for the next course to be served. Eventually it dawned on her that no other food was coming. Even the prom queen ate every speck of macaroni.

After a beat, Eric rubbed his stomach. "Ah, there's nothing like a full belly," he said sarcastically. "And that was *nothing* like a full belly. Who wants seconds?"

Daley gulped. "Nobody. That's all we get till tomorrow."

"But I'm starving here!" Eric protested.

"Naw, you're hungry," Daley answered. "When the food runs out, *then* you'll be starving."

Nathan shook his bushy mop of hair. "And when is that gonna be?"

Daley frowned and answered in a low voice, "Tomorrow. Unless we cut the portions in half and—"

"Half?" Eric shrieked. "That was nothing. You can't cut nothing in half. That's like . . . negative nothing."

Nathan smiled. "Not a math guy, are you?"

Daley paced across the sand, running her hands nervously through her red hair. "What can I say? The more we eat, the faster it goes."

"But we might get rescued by, like, tomorrow, right?" Taylor asked hopefully.

"Or eventually," Eric muttered, "which is 'never.'"

"Stop saying that!" Taylor snapped.

An argument began, with everyone yelling at the same time. Jackson rose to his full height and shouted, "Time!"

Everybody shut up at once, looking surprised by Jackson's tone. This was new for him. *Get used to it*, he thought, *since we gotta solve the food problem. Today*.

They watched him, waiting for the next lung to bellow. Jackson paced slowly, choosing his words carefully. "Two choices," he began. "We hunt for more food, or we starve."

The group exchanged worried glances, and Jackson picked up the weapon he'd been carving all day. It was only a sharpened stick, but he was sure that he could spear a fish with it. He had never tried to spear a fish—or anything else—but he had seen lots of TV shows on the nature channels.

He slapped the lance into his palm. "Today, we hunt."

TWO

The waves swirled around Jackson's legs. He had been out in the ocean for about fifteen minutes looking for fish. And so far, he hadn't seen a thing. Not even a guppy.

Jackson had gone through a phase when he was in middle school where he was into all these survival books—*The Swiss Family Robinson* and stuff like that. When the characters in the books got into trouble, they always worked out some ingenious solution that turned out great. There was one book about a family in Montana. The dad had quit his job in New York City or something, and the family went out and lived in a cabin with no electricity or anything. They hunted elk and deer, and they fished. The oldest kid had made a spear, and he'd go out in this stream and spear fish. In one chapter he speared like ten fish in one afternoon.

Sitting in his bedroom in the middle of L.A., it had all seemed really reasonable to Jackson. You got a stick. You sharpened the point. You practiced throwing it into the sand until you got your aim down. Then you went into the water where the fish lived and you speared a whole bunch of them. Easy.

But here on Reality Island, it didn't work like that. Jackson was starting to think that the book was totally bogus. The guy who wrote it was probably sitting around in his big mansion out in the suburbs of some city on the East Coast. He probably had never set foot in Montana, much less tried to spear some slippery fish with a dinky little stick.

And more importantly, where were the freakin' fish?

Here Jackson was in the middle of the freakin' ocean, which was where all the freakin' fish were supposed to live, and he'd been out here for like a whole freakin' hour—and how many fish had he seen?

Zero.

Zero freakin' fish.

Well, there had been a couple of glints of silver zipping through the water—tiny little fish about the size of your finger that went racing past about a million miles per hour. But that was it. You'd see this silver flash, and by the time you'd even lifted your spear—*ssshshhhhhheeeeooooow!*—that little bad boy was gone.

And even if he'd hit the thing, best he could tell, these fish were nothing but glorified minnows. You'd probably burn more calories catching it than you'd get from eating it.

Jackson couldn't quit, though. Back on the beach everybody was watching him. Not all at once, maybe—but every few minutes somebody would wander by and stare at him for a while. Once or twice he'd thrown his spear at nothing just to make it seem like he was at least *seeing* some fish out here.

He noticed Eric standing at the water's edge. Lazy jerk.

Eric gave him a big thumbs-up and his cheesiest grin. "Keep it up, O Fearless Leader!" Eric yelled.

Jackson ignored him. When he turned around again a few minutes later, Eric was lying in the sand sleeping.

Suddenly Jackson saw something. A dark thing moving in the water. An *enormous* dark thing.

Jackson felt a prickle on the back of his neck. Okay. Okay, maybe this was something. He lifted his spear slowly to his shoulder.

The dark thing moved slowly, then wheeled and disappeared.

What *was* that? Whatever it was, it was huge. It couldn't have been a whale, right? A manta ray?

A *shark*?

Nah, it was too big. Sharks didn't get that big. Right?

Jackson was not totally comfortable in the water to begin with. And now he was feeling nervous. Was his spear even strong enough to kill the thing?

He waited, a jittery tingling feeling running through his arms.

The water darkened for a moment again, then lightened. The thing seemed to be moving deeper into the water. Wait! There it was again! Man, it was big. The water was very clear and blue, but there was something strangely indistinct about this thing.

Jackson began following it, slogging heavily through the water. He was up to his chest now. Some of the waves were lifting him off his feet. Was he being crazy? Maybe he should stick closer to the shore.

He looked back at the beach. Whoa, he was getting pretty far out now. He felt a jolt of nervousness. The kids on the beach had gotten very small and distant. Part of him thought he should head back in.

But the thought of coming back empty-handed was worse than his fear of whatever was out there in the water. So he put the thing out of his mind and kept on looking.

Come on, fishies, he thought. *Come to papa.*

Much as he hated to do it, Nathan had to give their leader some credit. Jackson had gone straight into the water, wandering out beyond the breakers, hurling his makeshift spear at the fish. Time after time, he plunged the lance into the roiling surf and proudly lifted the weapon to find . . .

Nothing. Zip. Nada.

Nathan tried not to laugh, because he wasn't exactly catching any fish sitting on the beach. But still. The rest of the castaways poked sticks in the sand or brushed the bugs out of their hair while they glumly watched Jackson's efforts. It wasn't lifting anyone's spirits, and it looked as if they soon might have to rescue him from the undertow.

Eric shook his head and said, "Who's he kidding?"

"Isn't he a city guy?" Daley asked, pulling her unruly mass of red hair out from under her cap.

"Not a lot of spearfishing going on in the 'hood," Nathan said. *This would be really entertaining*, he decided, *if we weren't all starving*.

Melissa cocked her head and sighed, "But he looks good." That brought a bunch of quizzical glances. Melissa suddenly looked embarrassed. Nathan had a hunch that Melissa was getting the hots for the guy. Which seemed a little weird to him. Sweet little Melissa and Mr. Bad Boy? Nah, he didn't see it.

Eric kept watching, a little smirk on his face. "The only thing he's gonna spear is his foot."

"Well, I am *not* eating his foot," Taylor said.

Nathan had given up trying to figure out whether she was joking with comments like that. If she were acting, man, she ought to be in the movies.

Nathan turned his attention back to the fisherman. Jackson made an awkward lunge, sank into the surf up to his chest, then got knocked over by a second wave. For a second Nathan got worried: Jackson's head disappeared from view for what seemed an awfully long time. But then Jackson staggered to his feet, waving an empty spear—still alive . . . but defeated by a bunch of fish.

Nathan's stomach growled. It was all well and good watching Jackson battle it out with the waves. But it wasn't gonna feed anybody.

Food. Nathan tried to think of something they could eat. He looked back at the jungle. A tantalizing bunch of coconuts hung from a distant, tall palm. He'd already tried to get them down once and it hadn't gone very well. It was like they were laughing at him, taunting. Stupid coconuts. There was a whole meal hanging right there, not twenty-five feet in the air. It wasn't right, getting beat by a bunch of coconuts.

"What's that?" Eric interrupted Nathan's meditation on the coconuts. Eric was pointing at the water.

"That would be our fearless leader," Daley said, "stabbing the ocean to death."

"Nah, nah. Beyond him. That fin-looking thing sticking up out of the water."

Everybody looked to see what he was talking about. All Nathan could see were little waves. Nathan was surprised at just how far out Jackson had gotten.

"There's a sandbar out there," Lex said. "Now that it's low tide, you can stand up way out there."

"Wait, wait, wait," Daley said. "Fin? What kind of fin?"

Eric shrugged. "Oh, you know. Kind of like a big black triangle?"

"Where?"

Eric pointed. Nathan wasn't sure whether to take him seriously or not. Eric was so full of baloney, you never knew when to trust anything he said.

Still, everyone suddenly had their eyes glued to the water around Jackson. Jackson flailed around, not doing much now. He seemed to be looking for something, chasing it around a lot, but not using his spear at all. It looked like an awful lot of work.

And then suddenly there it was.

A large black fin rose up out of the waves. It couldn't have been more than fifty feet behind Jackson.

"Ohmygod!" Taylor said. "Is that a—"

Everyone looked at the water, then at one another.

"Shark!" Melissa started running toward the surf. "Jackson! Look out! There's a shark behind you!"

Nathan felt frozen. The shark—if that's what it was—was circling toward Jackson. Then, suddenly, it disappeared.

"Somebody *do* something!" Taylor said.

"*I'm* not going in there," Eric said.

Nathan jumped to his feet, followed Melissa to the edge of the water. "Jackson!" he yelled. "Look behind you!"

But Jackson was so far out now that he couldn't hear anything they were saying.

Jackson was pleasantly surprised to find that all of a sudden the water had gotten shallower. *There must be a sandbar out here*, he thought. As the water had gotten shallower, it had also gotten clearer. He could see the sand underneath his feet now. *If there are any fish out here, they're mine!*

He paused, scanned the water, looking for the dark shape again.

Suddenly, there it was. Bigger, darker, moving faster. It was the weirdest thing, though. It seemed almost shapeless, like a huge storm cloud moving around in the water. He wondered, once again, if this was such a brilliant idea. He looked back at the shore, curious to see how far out he'd come.

The other kids were lined up along the shore, waving at him. It was like they were giving him moral support or something. He grinned and waved his spear at them. It was kinda cool that they were all urging him on like that. Kinda nice. Kinda unexpected, too. These rich kids usually seemed too absorbed in themselves to pay attention to anything anybody else was doing.

He turned back toward the horizon.

The dark thing was gone. Wait! There! He lifted his spear.

And then he saw what it was. It wasn't one fish at all. It wasn't a shark or a whale or a manta ray. It was a whole school of fish! Thousands of them! Unbelievable. And they were moving right toward him!

He lifted his spear, feeling a wave of excitement and urgency run through his body. Yes! This was it. Finally!

He waited until they had reached him. They were sizable fish, each over a foot long. Just one would make a good meal. Maybe even enough for two people.

Suddenly he imagined himself coming back with dozens of fish, all the other kids awed by his skills. Where would he even put them all? In his pockets? In his shirt? *Okay, okay*, he thought. *Concentrate!*

The fish surged and writhed around him. He could feel

them bumping against his legs. They were swarming so fast and thick, he couldn't pick out an individual fish. But it hardly mattered, there were so many of them. He waited until they were all around him, then he plunged the spear into the midst of them, hurling it down with all his strength.

The spear impaled something, burying itself in the sand. Only about a foot of stick stuck out of the waves now.

And then, like that, they were gone. He looked at his spear, visible in the clear blue water, its point buried in the sand. It was kinda hard to see the fish he'd speared. In fact . . . he couldn't see it at all.

He gingerly pulled his stick out of the sand, trying hard not to lose whatever he'd impaled. He held it up.

What! He couldn't believe it. With like a million fish surging through the water around him, he'd missed. How was that even possible? He stared at the spear point. Well, bad luck, he supposed. Next time he'd get one for sure.

He looked around, saw the dark shape moving just beyond comfortable spear-throwing range. But that was okay. Once you had the knack for spotting the school of fish, you couldn't miss it. Boy, those fish were just racing around like crazy! They went one way, then another, then another, a torrent of fish, zooming this way and that, the whole school moving like it had one mind.

You almost got exhausted just watching them. He wondered why they seemed so frantic. You'd think they'd wear themselves out.

And then he was in the thick of them again. This time he couldn't miss! He waited until they were all around him, then flung the spear again.

"He can't hear us!" Melissa screamed. She could feel the pulse racing in her veins.

"Ohmygod! Ohmygod! Ohmygod!" Taylor kept saying it over and over again.

"I can't watch," Eric said. "The sight of blood makes me nauseated." He turned and walked quickly off toward the hulk of the downed airplane.

Nathan glared at him. "What is *wrong* with him?"

Daley dismissed him with a flick of her hand. "Forget him. We need to think of something."

"Jackson!" Nathan yelled, cupping his hands around his mouth. "Jacksooooooooonnnnnn!"

"Jackson!" Melissa screamed. "Look out!"

But Jackson didn't pay any attention at all. He was busy throwing his spear into the water. Behind him the fin appeared. Then a second one, this time even larger than the first. Then a third. Then a fourth.

"Ohmygod! Ohmygod!"

"We have to do *something*," Melissa said.

"Isn't there a flare pistol in 29 DWN?" Lex said. "Maybe we could shoot it over his head."

"By the time we find it, he'll be shark food," Daley snapped.

Without even thinking about it, Melissa plunged into the waves.

"Don't be stupid," Daley said. "It won't help him if they eat you, too."

"Mel!" Nathan shouted. "Mel, come back!"

But Melissa couldn't help herself. She just kept moving into the surging waves.

Four times now Jackson had hurled the spear into the mob of fish. And four times he'd come up with nothing. Once more he threw it desperately at the fish. It missed yet again, bobbed to the surface, and started floating away from him on the crest of a large wave.

The fish kept moving wildly around him. It really was weird how frantic they seemed.

And then Jackson realized why. He saw a black thing powering sinuously through the water not five feet behind the school of fish. A fin broke the surface. Man, that thing was big! Probably seven, eight feet long, moving as fast as a car under the water.

Jackson felt a cold sensation run through his veins.

The black thing sliced through the center of the school of fish—a dark, predatory shape moving effortlessly beneath the waves. The school momentarily broke in half, and then rejoined, flashing off in a different direction.

A cloud of red liquid hung lazily in the blue water. Whatever the black thing was, it had just killed one of the fish with a single snap of its jaws.

A wave rolled through, and the cloud of blood was gone. A fish head bobbed on the waves, but the rest of the body was gone, ripped away by the teeth of the black predator.

Jackson looked desperately at his spear. The waves had caught it and it was moving rapidly away from him into deeper water. He spotted the dark shape—fifteen yards away. Directly between him and his weapon. Jackson felt his pulse hammering in his veins.

The dark shape in the water slowed, hanging motionless in the water. Then it turned, slowly. It faced straight toward him, its tail moving lazily in the water.

And then, as though they had materialized out of thin air, he saw them.

They were all around him. One black shape here, another there, another there, circling slowly around him. A black, triangular fin broke the surface of the water.

And over there was his only defense against them—his spear, drifting gently on the waves, moving slowly away into the dark water.

Melissa was about a hundred yards into the water now. The tide must have been coming in because she was up to her neck, and the water was getting deeper. Each wave pulled her off her feet. She wasn't the world's strongest swimmer, and this was really starting to scare her.

But she was even more scared for Jackson.

She forged ahead. "Jackson!" she yelled. "Jackson, come back in!"

And then she noticed that he was just standing there, frozen, the water up to his waist. Somehow he'd lost his spear. And she could tell from the expression on his face that he'd seen them. She counted the fins.

One, two, three . . . seven of them. No wait, six? No, seven. They were everywhere!

"Jackson! Look out! Behind you!"

For the first time, he heard her. He whirled. "Go back!" he shouted. "Sharks! Go back!"

And as he shouted, he spotted one of the fins. It began moving toward him. First lazily, then gaining speed, going faster now, faster, heading straight for him.

"Look out!" she screamed.

Jackson felt a burst of anger. What was Melissa thinking? She'd obviously seen the sharks. So why had she come out here? She didn't exactly seem like the thrill-junkie type. Was she a total idiot?

And then he realized. That's why they'd been waving at him from the shore. Not to encourage him, but to tell him to get out of the water.

"Go back!" He flailed at the air, indicating that she should swim back. A wave crashed over her head, and for a moment, she disappeared.

Then another fin surfaced in the water about fifty yards in front of Jackson. It seemed like he could feel the animals out there, watching him.

They kept moving. Straight toward him. Faster, faster.

He couldn't believe how fast the black shapes moved. He felt so clumsy and slow in the water, but the sharks moved with blinding efficiency. A strange thought crossed his mind as the predators accelerated toward him: If they weren't so deadly, the stupid monsters would be really beautiful.

Closer, closer, faster, faster the animals swam. And there was not a shadow of a doubt now: They were heading straight for him.

Why had he thrown the spear away like that? Stupid! Trying to hit some dumb fish that must have been twenty feet away. It was just ego. Trying to impress a bunch of rich kids he barely even knew.

What had he been thinking?

Closer, faster. The fins were heading straight toward him.

He drew his arm back. Maybe he could punch one of them in the nose or something. At least he'd go down fighting.

Closer. Closer.

"Look out!" He could hear Melissa's voice now. "Jackson, look out!"

And just as the sharks had reached a point not ten feet from him, he felt this weird sensation—like, okay, maybe this was it . . . but he was okay with it. Here he was, a poor kid from a crappy neighborhood, his first time in the ocean—and he was about to turn into dinner for a couple of sharks. Well, most of his homies from the old neighborhood—living not five miles from the ocean—probably would never go swimming in the Pacific in their whole lives. So maybe this wasn't such a bad way to go.

And then they were on him.

From the shore Daley yelled, "Look out!" She knew as she screamed that it would do no good at all.

"Ohmygodohmygodohmygod!" Taylor's words had turned into a chant now.

The fins raced closer and closer.

And then something bizarre happened.

Jackson stumbled backward, fell into the surf, waiting for the sickening impact.

But instead of dozens of razor-sharp teeth locking onto his leg, something entirely unexpected happened.

Something magical.

The sharks burst out of the water. And flew through the air.

And as they rose into the air and sailed over his head, the sharks changed color, changed form, changed shape.

Jackson felt relief shoot through his veins.

Sharks? No, they had never been sharks.

They were dolphins!

The big creatures sailed over his head and smacked back into the water with a huge splash. Droplets of water hung like diamonds in the air, then rained down on his head.

Jackson began to laugh.

Melissa began struggling up out of the water and onto the sandbar. She was laughing now, too.

They stood in the middle of the water next to each other, watching as the playful mammals circled them, leaping out of the water and into the air.

Melissa laughed so hard that after a minute tears started running down her face. Her hair was matted to her head and her clothes were streaming with water.

"Oh, man," she said, finally catching her breath. "I'm feeling a little weird."

She collapsed into Jackson's arms and began to giggle again.

"Dolphins," she said. "I can't believe it. They're just dolphins."

She felt warm against him. Suddenly she stiffened. "God, I'm sorry," she said. "I didn't mean to . . ."

"No, no," Jackson said. "Thanks for coming out to warn me."

She jerked away from him, looking embarrassed. Then she smoothed out her soaked shirt. "So . . ." she said.

Jackson watched the dolphins. The school of fish they had been chasing suddenly made a break for the deep water and, like that, the dolphins disappeared, following their meal out into the depth of the ocean.

"So," she said again. "All this swimming. Kinda makes you hungry, huh?"

"Yeah," Jackson said. Jackson was feeling it, too. Now that the excitement was past, his stomach felt hollow.

"I don't suppose you caught anything for supper?"

Jackson cleared his throat sheepishly. His spear was now bobbing along about a hundred yards away.

"Uh . . ." he said.

THREE

After it appeared that the whole thing had been a total false alarm—the "sharks" had turned out to be nothing but dolphins—Nathan slipped away from the others and went to the tent where the video camera was set up on a tripod. As long as Taylor kept the batteries charged from the solar panel, they were all free to keep a video diary.

Nathan

Well, that was kinda scary. We thought Jackson was a goner. He was out there trying to spear a fish. Then all these sharks showed up and Mel goes running out into the waves trying to save him.

Who'da thunk it, huh? I wouldn't have thought she had it in her. Anyway, now that the scares are over, it's like, man, he's been out there for hours practically giving himself a hernia throwing that spear. And he's got nothing.

So let's get real. No way Jackson's gonna get any fish. Which means I've gotta pick up the slack and step up my hunt for fruit. I know where there's a bunch of it, but that means I've gotta return to the scene of the crime. I've got to suck it up and go back to face—

"Face what?" Daley asked. She stepped around the corner of the tent and peered at him.

He looked at her grimly and nodded his head. "You know what. Get your little brother and come with me, but don't tell anyone else."

In a clearing not far from the edge of the island's jungle stood a monstrous coconut palm tree. The granddaddy of all coconut palms. It made the Empire State Building look like a shack. Nathan put out of his mind how tall it was—he concentrated on a bunch of big coconuts at the top. It was enough to feed them all for at least a week. Well, maybe that was exaggerating. But he'd definitely be a total hero if he got them down.

Problem was, he'd tried climbing it before. And he'd fallen off—and just about killed himself.

The question was . . . *How do I get them down? Without nearly killing myself, like I almost did last time?* It was all about technique. There had to be a way.

"Lotta coconuts up there," Lex admitted. "*Waaayy* up there." The ten-year-old shook his head doubtfully.

"How far up did you get when you fell?" Daley asked.

Nathan squared his shoulders and answered, "Doesn't matter. I'm not falling again."

"Maybe we should look someplace else," Lex suggested.

"No. I am all over this." Nathan rubbed his hands together and took a step closer to the trunk of the palm tree. This tree had the most coconuts of any tree he'd seen yet. So if he could conquer this one, he could handle any of them.

"Yeah, you will be," Daley said with one of her standard skeptical little chuckles, "after you go *splat*."

Nathan scowled at Daley. "Aren't you supposed to be rationing food or something?" he asked her.

"Sure, as soon as you get us some." She gave him a bland smile.

It was exactly the encouragement he needed. Daley was totally *not* gonna tell him what he could or couldn't do. Nathan ripped off his shirt and stared up at the massive tree. *They can cut on me all they want*, he decided, *but I'm bringing home the coconuts. Even if it kills me.*

⊁

Taylor sang to herself while she worked. The sooner she got done with her crummy chores, the sooner she could move on to more important stuff. Like getting a tan. Maybe everyone else thought their vacation was over, but this still looked like a tropical paradise to her. A cheap one, maybe. But still, Captain What's-His-Name would be back any moment with the rescue team, and the helicopters would come to airlift them to the real paradise.

She would probably get on the national TV news, because they liked cute blondes. Taylor could picture it all in her mind. But before she did any work, she would have to do her video journal. She had to commit her thoughts for posterity, of course—while they were still fresh her mind. After some primping in her compact mirror, Taylor turned on the camera and sat in front of it.

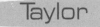
Taylor

We all have jobs, but mine is the most important. If not for me, we'd lose touch with the civilized world and go completely, like, Tarzan or something. It's a huge responsibility, but I will not let anyone down, no matter what.

Taylor paused the camera for a moment while she attached the leads of the battery charger to the terminals of the big red battery from the plane. Then she positioned the solar panel so that it faced the morning sun.

Charging batteries . . . check.

It was really important that she keep doing the video diary—even though it was kind of a pain in the neck. "I will not let anyone down, no matter what." That was a nice touch, huh? When they got back to California, that video was going to be her ticket to the big time. She could sell it to one of those TV news programs like *Entertainment Tonight* or whatever, and then wait for the movie offers to roll in. Blond girl on a desert island? Courageously saving the other kids from certain disaster? Just the right amount of tanned skin showing? Shut *up*—it was total money, no doubt about it.

Now it was time to examine the mp3 player that Lex had attached to speakers on top of the wrecked airplane. It was still charged, so she pushed a tiny button and unleashed the song "Let's Get It Started," which boomed across the beach. That was more like it! Everybody was all moping around and stressing. Come *on!* They needed to lighten up.

Entertainment . . . check.

Taylor danced around a little, swinging her hips. Felt kinda good to shake it. She looked around to see if anybody was checking her out. But nobody was watching. And what was the point of doing anything if there was nobody to watch you do it?

Taylor smoothed out her beach towel on the sand.

Rest after a job well done . . . check!

With a grin, she flicked off the camera, stretched out on her towel, and picked up her magazine. That had been grueling work, but she had the rest of the day to recover . . . thankfully.

Feeling half-drowned and completely waterlogged, Jackson staggered out of the ocean and toward his towel. How come it always worked so well in the movies?

Maybe they have better spears. Or slower fish.

He collapsed onto his towel and tried to catch his breath. That's when he noticed a small plastic container lying beside him. It had his name written on it in big, bold letters: *JACKSON.*

He looked around but didn't see anyone watching

him. They had all left him alone with his lousy fishing and utter embarrassment, so it was hard to say how long this box had lain here. *Whoever gave it to me . . . wanted me to open it in private.*

So he did. Inside the box were a couple of crude fishing hooks that looked as if they had been made out of earring hoops. There was also a note written on a small piece of yellow paper. For sure, that would tell him.

Jackson unfolded the note and read, *Lose the spear.* It was written in block letters with a red pen and signed, *A friend.*

He looked at the hooks again, then all around the beach. The others were off doing . . . whatever they were doing— their duties, he hoped. This anonymous buddy had given him some pretty good advice, but who was it? Probably Lex. Who else in this bunch knew anything practical?

I can't go fishing with just hooks, he thought. *I need a line, too.* What kind of string could he find that would be strong enough to reel in a fish?

Suddenly music blasted across the sand, and he turned and looked in its direction. He saw the speakers on top of the wrecked plane. He'd seen Lex wandering off into the jungle with Nathan and Daley, so it obviously wasn't Lex who had turned it on. He didn't mind Lex messing with his mp3 player. But not anybody else.

Despite being cold and hungry and worn out, Jackson headed for the plane. He ducked under the wing and nearly tripped over Taylor, who was sunning herself like a tourist on a cruise ship. *Figures,* he thought. Miss Party Girl. She was probably the worst of the whole bunch. Her rich old man spent most of his free time dumping expensive goodies on her, so she thought she owned the whole world.

Taylor was the last one he felt he had to please. He

glanced over to make sure she was still charging the batteries, and that the solar panel was positioned okay. *At least she knows how to catch rays.*

Jackson jumped onto the wing of the plane, making a loud bump. Taylor cracked open one eye and said, "What are ya doing?"

Without a word, he climbed up to the top of the fuselage and began ripping away the speaker wire. The music died an abrupt death. Taylor's mouth fell open. "Excuse *me*," she said. "That's *my* music. I'm listening to that."

When he ignored her, she sat up.

"I'll have you know, I'm playing it for everybody. I'm, like, doing *extra* work, okay? I'm keeping everybody's spirits up."

He started pulling long loops of wire off the wing, finally detaching them from the speakers completely.

"Hey!" she said as he walked away. "I'm talking to you!"

He kept walking, spooling the long strand of wire around his arm.

"But I can't live without music," she yelled.

Here's a quarter, Jackson thought. *Call someone who cares.*

Nathan swatted a mosquito away from his face and gazed upward. He could almost hear a chorus singing when he looked at the monster palm tree and its inviting coconuts.

This is survival time, he told himself. *We need that food, and I have to get psyched to get it!*

Grunting and rustling noises broke his concentration, and he turned to see Lex and Daley piling fallen palm fronds around the trunk. It was obvious what they were doing, but he figured he'd make it hard on them anyway.

"Hey, what's that for, Daley?" he snapped.

"For when you fall," Daley answered. She didn't add, "Well, duh," but he could hear it in her voice.

"I'm not gonna fall," he said calmly.

He braced one foot on the tree, then began to climb. Unfortunately, he got only a few feet before he lost his grip and slid down, scraping his hands and knees.

"You don't have to do this," Daley said.

"What's the problem?" Nathan said. He knew he wasn't really angry at Daley. He was angry at this tree. At the situation. At their helplessness. Somebody had to prove that the seven remaining survivors could overcome the odds against them. And Nathan figured he might as well be the one to prove it. But it didn't help to have Daley standing there with her hands on her hips, ready to bombard him with "helpful" criticism.

Plus, all he had proven so far was that he could fall down trees and lose elections. That wasn't Nathan McHugh, though. Nathan McHugh was no loser. Nathan McHugh was a pacesetter, a winner, a leader.

Problem was, he had yet to prove it.

The proof was hanging right there at the top of this tree . . . if only he could reach it.

F**O**UR

At the fire pit, under a crude canopy of old canvas, Melissa sat tending her fire and the camp pot, set on a tripod of fire-hardened sticks. She added some wood and stirred up the flames, thinking how this really was very meditative and relaxing work . . . purifying the water.

Melissa

Everybody's stressing about food. I can't blame them. I'm hungry, too. And our food's not going to last much longer. But we've got to be careful. We don't have hospitals or ambulances or doctors here. If somebody gets hurt trying to get food, then it's not worth it.

Today Jackson went out to try spearing fish, and we thought he was surrounded by sharks, and then I went flying out into the water, too. Which is weird, because that's so not me. I'm not exactly the bold adventurer type of girl. But I just got so scared for Jackson that I couldn't stop myself.

I don't know what it is about him. There's just something about him that makes me feel all—okay, okay, I'll shut up about that before I say something all corny and stupid.

Anyway, lucky for me, I've got a job that I kind of enjoy.

Food's important, of course, but so is water. Since I'm in charge of keeping the fire going, I'm also in charge of filtering the water through cloth and boiling it to make sure it's safe to drink. It's actually kind of fun! I just sit here on the beach and do my thing and it feels nice when I'm done. Like I've accomplished something.

Melissa picked up the camera, lifted the pot lid, and filmed the bubbling water. *If we ever get rescued, maybe this will get me extra credit in biology or something.*

Melissa flicked off the camera and turned her attention to the jungle path. Okay, where was Eric? Eric was supposed to be her assistant. But Eric—he was a funny guy and everything—but, well . . . not so great when it came to getting stuff done. She'd been sitting here for a while and suddenly she realized he was awfully late with the latest batch of well water. It was always damp, misty, and buggy over there where the well was—with lots of leeches. She hoped Eric was all right.

She sighed. Better go find out what he was doing.

How did I get this lousy job? Eric wondered. *I did not sign up to be Melissa's pack mule.*

For what seemed like the tenth time that day, he had to fill two big plastic water jugs with well water. Sure, it sounded easy, but the "well" was just a muddy hole crawling with leeches. To get the water out, all he had was this crummy little plastic cup. Once he filled the cup, he had to carefully pour each cupful through a makeshift funnel until he got the two big jugs completely filled. With water, not leeches.

Then came the hard part, the mule part. He had to carry both jugs, one in each hand, all the way back to the fire pit. Sometimes they were too heavy, and he had to empty a little of the water back into the well. It took forever to get the weight distribution just right, and even then he still strained his back . . . and every other muscle he had!

This is getting old.

Eric wanted to make a video diary showing all the miserable work he was doing, but he would need a cameraman for that. The others were all off doing their cushy, fun jobs . . . all of them *way* easier than his. Like that little slacker, Lex, whose only job was to think of brilliant stuff to do with all the junk they had saved from the plane.

That should be my job, Eric decided. *I can think way better than any of those overachievers. Besides, doesn't somebody have to be the comedian, to keep everyone's spirits up? Doesn't somebody have to make sure Taylor is okay . . . that she's comfortable enough? These are the important gigs.*

Action Jackson spends all day monkeying around in the ocean with his toy spear, pretending he's fishing, comes out with nothing but sand in his teeth, and everyone's all, "Oh, Jackson's so brave and diligent!" Whereas I'm killing myself, working like a slave for something that's actually productive and important. And what do I get for a reward?

The big zippo. Nothing. No respect, no reward, no nice back massage from Taylor. Zero.

There is definitely something wrong with this picture.

Eric lugged two half-filled bottles back to camp and stopped to rest at the edge of the jungle. On the beach—under a canopy in the shade—sat Melissa, poking at her precious fire. *Another really tough job*, Eric thought through clenched teeth.

Suddenly, he had an idea.

Time to stop thinking like a sucker. Abruptly, Eric switched from walking to limping. He hobbled like a wounded soldier. Unfortunately, Melissa's back was to him, so she couldn't see. *Time to throw a little audio into the mix.*

"Ouchhhhhh! Ahhhh! Oooh!"

Melissa whirled around, and Eric began wailing in earnest. He clutched one bare foot and hopped on the other, laying it on fairly thick.

"What happened?" she said, looking at him with her usual wide-eyed stare.

He staggered toward the fire pit and collapsed at her side. "I stepped on a pricker or something," he answered glumly. "Then I dove back and wrenched my ankle. Owww, man!"

Nice one.

"I'll get the first-aid kit," Melissa offered.

Eric pulled his foot back and put on a brave face. "No,

no, no . . . that's okay. The ankle hurts a lot more than the sharp thing. I can't let it stop me. We need water."

"Don't be dumb," Melissa said with a friendly smile. "You boil the water. I'll go lug it."

Perfecto, Eric thought. Instead he said, "But that's not your job."

"It's okay," she answered. "We gotta cover for each other." Melissa emptied the water jugs into her cooking pot and got ready to make the next run.

Eric didn't have to pretend to be thankful, because he was. "Well . . . I guess. Thank you, Melissa. You're a real team player."

"Stay off the foot," she ordered as she picked up the two empties and headed into the jungle.

"Oh, I will," Eric assured her. With a contented smile, he stretched out on Melissa's towel. *I definitely will.*

He practiced his tortured moans little. *Ohhhh. Uhhhnnggg. AGHHghghhhh.*

After a minute Taylor's voice drifted over the airplane. "Puh-lease! Enough with the phony whining, Eric. Melissa's not here to hear you."

Point taken, Eric thought. He picked up his towel and ran over to lie down next to her.

"Go away, Eric," she said. "You're distracting me."

"From what?"

She lay facedown, motionless on the sand. "I'm concentrating on my tan."

He stared at her. Was she serious?

"And stop staring at my butt."

He blinked. How did she know? Defeated, he sighed and walked back over to the fire. Man, he couldn't catch a break to save his life. He spread out the towel and lay down again.

Nathan sat on the ground, moping. Maybe he could sprout wings and fly up that coconut tree. Best he could tell, that was the only way up the thing. They didn't have an ax big enough to chop it down. They didn't have a ladder. They didn't have—

When he heard distant voices, he jumped to his feet and rubbed dirt on his hands, as if he were just about to charge straight up that trunk.

Daley and Lex emerged from the jungle, looking hot and sweaty. *What have they been doing?* Nathan wondered.

It seems like everyone is still keeping secrets. Trying to get an edge on everyone else. How can we hope to pull off this survival stuff with everybody running their own show? As long as Daley just wants to make fun of me, I'm not going to pay any attention to her. My only problem is how to get the coconuts down from that stupid tree.

He sat on the ground and began to take off his boots. Daley shook her head and said, "Nathan, seriously. Give it up. We've got a whole—"

"It's cool," he said, cutting her off. "I got a Plan B."

"For bare feet?" asked Daley.

"Ha! Cute," he answered, taking off his socks. "But yeah. It's how the locals do it."

"Local what? The island is deserted."

"Maybe you should find a smaller tree," Lex suggested.

I'm not giving up yet, Nathan thought. *Or ever!* He jumped to his feet and looked up at the stately palm. "This is gonna work," he insisted. "It's all about the traction."

Nathan wrapped his arms around the tree trunk and began to climb. He was going up, but the spines and prickles in the craggy bark were gouging the bottoms of his bare feet.

"Ow . . . ouch! Pain!" he cried, trying to hold on. "Rough tree, tender feet. Not good. Owww!" For once, he was really glad to fall off.

Daley tried not to laugh, but Lex gave a chuckle. "I guess the locals have tougher feet," he said.

"Or ladders," Daley added.

Nathan hobbled off, trying not to show how much pain he was in. Or how embarrassed. If he didn't figure out a way to climb that tree soon, he would waste a whole day *and* look like an idiot. Plus, they really needed those coconuts.

He turned around to see Lex headed for the beach and Daley going back into the jungle. *What are they up to?*

Eric wasn't at all bored just sitting around because there was a lot of entertainment on the beach. Over near the plane, Taylor continued sunbathing. Always nice eye candy. Out in the surf, Jackson was fishing. At least he was doing something with a pole that *looked* like fishing, although he spent most of his time trying to untangle his line. Kinda pathetic. Poor guy had been out there in the water for hours—first the spearfishing, now the miserable-looking fishing pole.

Empty-handed, Jackson finally gave up and headed to the fire pit, shivering slightly. Eric felt a little guilty, because— for real—the big guy looked pretty ragged out. But he was more concerned about Melissa, who came lumbering out of the jungle with full water bottles. Eric frowned and rubbed his ankle, trying to remember that he was in pain. He made sure to stoke the fire with more wood, then poke around in the flames with a stick like he was some All-Pro fire tender.

Gotta look like I'm working hard, Eric thought. *I'm conserving my energy, while the rest of them are wasting theirs. After we're rescued, nobody will remember what anybody did. Or didn't do.*

With a scowl, Jackson walked up to the fire, threw down his stick, and put his hands out to the fire. His fingers were shriveled up like prunes from spending half the day in the water. "Hey, Chief," Eric said, "any bites?"

The only answer he got was a cold stare.

"Never mind," Eric said cheerfully. "You'll get there." He heard a grunt, and he turned around to see Melissa setting down the water bottles. *Man, that girl can haul some water*. He wondered if she'd saved the strength to work the kinks out of his sore muscles. He was about to ask, but she looked right past him and smiled sympathetically at Jackson.

"Maybe you should try a different kind of bait," she said.

Jackson blinked at her as if he'd been hit in the head with a propeller. "Bait?" he muttered.

Eric tried not to laugh.

Muttering to himself, Jackson grabbed his fishing pole and stomped off.

"So much for seafood," Eric said.

Melissa watched him go. "You think I shouldn't have said that?"

"Hey, if the guy's fishing and he's not using bait, then he needs to go back to the drawing board, huh?"

"I guess you're right." Looking miserable over embarrassing their leader, Melissa inspected the fire and the cooking pot. The fire was burning, and the water was boiling, just like it was supposed to. *Piece of cake.*

"Hey, great," Melissa said with relief. "How many bottles did you fill?"

Eric squinted at her. "I was supposed to fill bottles?"

"That's the whole point," Melissa said, flapping her arms. "After you filter the water, you boil it and put it in the bottles to cool."

"I was supposed to filter the water?" Eric asked with a gulp.

"Eric!" she shrieked.

"Sorry, I wasn't thinking straight." He made a big show of rubbing his ankle. "It's the pain, you know? But I'm on it now, I swear."

Melissa looked doubtfully at him, but Eric knew there was nothing she could do. *This is my job now,* Eric thought. *If you don't like your job, steal somebody else's.*

Glumly Mel picked up two empty jugs and got ready to make another trip to the well. Eric watched her as she shuffled back into the jungle and out of sight. Then he watched Jackson digging in the mud near the tree line, apparently looking for worms. Taylor was in full pout, arms crossed, staring lightning bolts at Jackson.

My dad would love this, Eric thought. Eric's old man was a comedy writer, always getting a good laugh when other people's lives got all fouled up. All these kids hustling around, all full of self-importance and drama—the old guy would love it. For godsake, how could you get excited about filtering *water*? He'd get a chuckle out of that. Of course, when things got screwed up in his *own* life, his dad never thought it was so hilarious. And come to think of it, the gnawing emptiness in the stomach was not such a laugh riot. Or the bug bites and the sand fleas, or sleeping on the ground in a leaky tent.

Well, what were you gonna do? You're stuck here, you

might as well make the best of it. Have a few laughs.

As long as it doesn't last too long.

Jackson dug for worms for about half an hour but found nothing. The soil was really sandy and thin. Maybe they just didn't have earthworms here. Did fish eat bugs? God knows they had enough of *them* around here.

He caught a few little creepy-crawlies that were meandering around in the litter of palm fronds and leaves on the ground and put them in a plastic bag. But by the time he got four or five of them, the first two bugs he'd put in the bag had crawled out. It wasn't a zip-top bag, so there was no way to seal it.

I could be at this all day, he thought wearily. It was getting later and later, and he still hadn't even had a nibble.

Suddenly, he had a brainstorm.

He stood up and walked past the fire, where Eric was busy pretending to be busy—while, in fact, doing nothing. Jackson headed into the jungle, shaking his head. If that guy put half the energy into doing actual work as he did into trying to shirk it, he'd get all kinds of stuff done.

After a short walk down the little trail that was rapidly being worn into the ground between the beach and the clearing, Jackson reached the well.

Melissa was just finishing filling up her second jug.

"I thought you were fire," he said.

Melissa looked up. "Yeah, well, Eric hurt his foot, so I thought I'd help him out."

Jackson snorted.

"What? You think he's not hurt?"

Jackson just shook his head sadly.

"But ..." Melissa frowned. "He was moaning and limping and everything. You don't think he'd *lie* about something like that ... do you?"

Jackson gave her a look, like *You're kidding, right?* Then he plopped down next to the well.

"Oh." Melissa flushed. "Now I feel silly."

Jackson leaned over, put his arm in the water, all the way up to the elbow. He could see little wiggly things moving around in the mucky water.

"Um, Jackson?"

He looked up at Melissa.

"Um. You know there are leeches in there?"

Jackson smiled. "Exactly."

This isn't working.

The leeches had seemed like a stroke of genius. Fish liked worms, right? And leeches were worms. Therefore, leeches should be perfect bait, right? It was plain old simple logic, Jackson had figured.

But noooooo!

He had spent another forty-five minutes getting knocked around by the surf, and as far as he could tell, the fish had shown zero interest in leeches. Once again—total strike-out, total waste of time. He reeled in his fishing line and found the hook empty. *Maybe this just isn't my gig*, he decided. He headed back to shore.

Jackson was so tired that he could barely stand on his feet. And he was freezing, too. Even though it was a very warm day, the water just seemed to suck the heat out of his body. Every time he'd gone in, he'd gotten cold faster. His teeth were actually chattering this time. Must have been eighty-five, ninety degrees outside, and still he was freezing his butt off. He considered standing near the fire. But he was exhausted, too. He figured maybe he'd kill two birds with one stone: If he crawled into his sleeping bag, he could take a nap and warm up at the same time. He shuffled wearily to the boys' tent. As he pulled back the tent flap, Lex charged out, carrying some old clothes.

"Hey! How's the fishing?" Lex asked.

Jackson tried to will himself to be patient. He took a deep breath and plowed into the tent, collapsing onto his sleeping bag. Every muscle and bone in his body was screaming with exhaustion, but he couldn't get comfortable. He felt around under his sleeping bag, realizing that he was lying on something hard and lumpy. Under the bedding, he found another plastic box with his name on it.

What's this? More Fishing for Dummies! *Who the heck is leaving me these notes?*

He looked outside. Lex had just left the tent. He wondered why Daley's bro didn't just tell him what to do—Lex had never been shy about giving advice before.

Then again, maybe it wasn't Lex. But who else could it be? The whole thing left Jackson stumped.

With a weary sigh, Jackson opened the box and read the enclosed note. "Forget the surf," it said. "Fish like rocks and tide pools." It was written on the same kind of yellow paper as the first note, the same red pen, the same block letters. And like the first note it was signed, "A friend."

Suddenly he felt a surge of enthusiasm.

Okay, that made sense! Out in the surf, the undertow was too fast, and the fish had too much room to escape. In a tide pool, they were trapped. Plus the tide pools weren't that deep either, so he'd be able to warm up in the sun. Jackson staggered to his feet and was surprised to find that he had some more energy left. He grabbed his fishing gear and strode out of the tent. There were still a few hours of daylight left, and he didn't want to face the others empty-handed.

Empty hands meant empty stomachs.

Jackson looked down the beach, trying to figure out which one of these pampered rich kids knew anything about fishing.

Maybe it wasn't Lex after all. Truth was, he honestly had no idea.

FIVE

Daley stood near the palm tree, arms crossed, watching Nathan and her brother work.

She was getting frustrated. This insane climbing stunt had gone way too far. Now her little brother was involved—he had gotten a bunch of rags and was showing Nathan how to tie them around his ankles. Lex was actually *encouraging* Nathan to break his neck! *What's with that?*

It was bad enough that Nathan should break his neck, but he was going to fall on Lex and hurt him, too!

Daley stood off to the side, watching them with growing anger. Like a little professor, Lex explained his crazy idea. "This is how the Polynesians do it. Wrap the shirt around your feet and use it to grip the tree. Then you can shimmy up with your arms."

"How do you know these things?" Daley asked, shaking her head. The crazy thing was, this new scheme might work to get Nathan halfway up, but he was never going to get all the way to the top. Actually, the better it worked, the worse things would be in the long run. It would just mean he'd be that much higher when he finally fell off. He'd already fallen the other day and knocked himself out. This time he might do some serious damage.

Nathan carefully knotted the shirt around his ankles, leaving enough slack to go around the trunk of the tree. "I can do this," he said.

"News flash: You're not Polynesian," Daley declared. "This is idiotic."

"It's not," Nathan said. "This is sort of how I climbed up before."

"Then I *know* it's idiotic."

"But I used my arms to grab instead of my legs," he insisted. "This will work better." He gazed at her as if she was supposed to understand.

But she didn't. "Nathan, don't be dumb," Daley said. "You don't have to do this."

He looked pointedly at her and said through clenched teeth, "Yes ... I ... do."

"He really wants to do it," Lex told her.

"Obviously." Daley said softly, "He's gonna kill himself, and you just showed him how. Congratulations, Lex. Nice work. Maybe you could run back to the tent and work on the speech you're going to give his parents when you explain how you got their son killed."

"You're so funny," Nathan said. "Anyway, seriously, this is no big deal."

Lex shook his head. "It's gonna work, Nathan, but it's still pretty dangerous."

"I'm getting those coconuts," Nathan said. "If only to prove to Daley that I can."

"Or maybe to prove it to yourself," she answered.

For a minute Nathan looked like he was going to argue with her, but then he didn't. Probably because he knew she was right. She and Nathan didn't agree on very much, but she didn't want to see him hurt . . . or worse.

Nathan finished tying his feet to the tree trunk, and Lex inspected the knots and gave him a thumbs-up. Daley tried not to strangle both of them. She had a very bad feeling about this stunt. Even so, she had to admit that it would be harder for him to fall off the tree if he was tied to it. But that still didn't make it a good idea. *Why are guys so macho?*

When Nathan vaulted up the trunk, got a good grip, and began to shimmy, Daley had to look away. He was either going to conquer that tree or let it conquer him.

If he breaks a leg and can't be of any help, I'll kill him myself!

With her foot, Taylor adjusted the solar panel to catch more rays. She never even had to move an inch off her towel. *I've got this job down*, she told herself. *I'm pure efficiency. Nothing can stop the batteries from charging while I'm on duty.*

Too bad Jackson had helped himself to her speaker wire! What was that all about anyway?

Taylor could figure out most boys pretty fast, but not him. *Oh well.* He was cute, but he had a reputation. He probably wasn't worth the trouble. Bad boys were always way too much work. Plus, he was a *scholarship student*. Gross! She stretched out on her towel again and picked up her magazine. It was a good thing she never traveled without proper reading material, although she might have to read some of these articles twice . . . if they weren't rescued soon.

Suddenly a drop of water hit her back.

She turned her head, looked up at the sky. No clouds at all—clear and sunny. Weird.

Taylor went back to reading, and a few more drops hit her. She tried to ignore the raindrops until a downpour washed over her. Sputtering, Taylor jumped up and saw Eric leaning over the wing of the plane, a water bottle in his hand. She had to keep one hand behind her back to keep her bikini top from coming off.

"Wow, these tropical storms come out of nowhere!" he said. Giving her his usual little wiseacre grin.

"You are such a dirtbag!" she yelled at him.

Eric laughed innocently. "Aw, c'mon! You were working so hard, you need to cool off."

Taylor tried to slap him with her wet magazine, but having to keep her bikini top on with one hand slowed her down a little. Eric ducked and rolled off the wing. As soon as he hit the sand, he spotted something in the distance and said, "Uh-oh."

Before she could beat him up, he scampered off, hopping on one foot as he tried to pull off his shoe. He just barely managed to get back to the fire pit before Melissa staggered out of the jungle, hauling more water.

Taylor shook her head in amazement. She wasn't sure which amazed her more—how ridiculously over-the-top his performance was . . . or the fact that Melissa actually fell for it. She wondered if she should tell Melissa that she was being scammed. *Nah. Pffff. Not my problem.*

Taylor sat back down, looked over at her watch, which lay on the sand next to her towel. For a panicky moment she realized she hadn't been keeping track of the time. Hadn't it been about fifteen minutes that she'd been lying on her back? Time to turn over. There was literally nothing on the planet that was more disgusting than an uneven tan. Well, other than maybe leeches.

She rolled over, closed her eyes, and leaned back into the sunlight.

Exhausted, Melissa dropped the full water bottles onto the sand by the fire, then took a moment to study Eric. He looked as if he was doing the job—at least he was pouring water into their drinking bottles.

"I got it working now," he bragged. "I had to study the situation a little and come up with a system. That's why it looks like I didn't get too much done while you were gone. But now that I've, uh, engineered a system . . ." He snapped his fingers. "It's gonna go like *that*."

"Great," she breathed. "How's your foot?"

He lifted his chin bravely and answered, "Oh . . . it's okay. I guess."

Melissa didn't like being suspicious of people. It made her feel tired and nervous. "Look, I have to ask . . ." she said.

Eric cocked his head slightly, shifted his weight, wincing like it had hurt him just to move.

"You didn't, um, make this up, did you?" she said. "The hurt foot, I mean?"

Eric blinked, looking slightly offended. "Hey, look, no, forget it. You tend the fire, I'll get the water." Eric grabbed two empty water bottles that lay next to the fire and started hobbling awkwardly toward the woods. After he'd gone a stride or two, he stumbled and sprawled on the ground.

"Unnggg!" He seemed to be stifling a moan.

The water bottles flew off in opposite directions,

clattering on the dead palm fronds on the ground. Eric got slowly to his knees, jaw clenched and wincing, and started crawling toward the nearest water bottle. A tiny groan escaped from his mouth each time he moved.

Melissa felt terrible. He really seemed to be in a lot of pain. She ran over and tried to help him to his feet.

"I'm *fine*," Eric said, pushing her away. "Don't even worry about it."

Melissa let go of his arm, grabbed the nearest bottle. "Don't be like that," she said.

"Look, hey, it's nothing." He stumbled to his feet, winced again as he leaned over to pick up the other empty bottle. She snatched it from his hand.

"Please. Eric. Just stay off your foot."

Eric looked at her for a minute, then flopped down on the sand, shoulders slumped, looking completely defeated. "I feel like such a burden, Melissa. I want to pull my weight, but . . ." He put one hand over his eyes, like he was about to cry.

"Hey, look, purifying the water's a really important job. So is keeping the fire going."

He took his hand slowly away from his face, looked up at her with wide eyes. "You think so?"

She nodded, surveyed the area. He hadn't exactly gotten a lot of water purified. But at least he'd gotten a couple of squeeze bottles filled. She couldn't stand around and babysit him, though. *Someone* had to draw the water from the well.

"Hang in there, Eric. Okay?"

He swallowed. "I'll try," he said.

With a sigh, she picked up the empties and staggered back into the jungle.

After Melissa was gone, Eric heard a sound—a very slow, languid slapping noise. *Clap. Clap. Clap. Clap.* He looked over and saw Taylor clapping her hands together. Was it somehow possible to applaud sarcastically? She lay on her back, eyes closed behind her sunglasses, her face expressionless.

"Thank yew." Eric did his best Elvis impression. "Thank yew vurrry much!"

He stood, started to grab his towel and scurry over to lie down next to her.

"Don't even *think* about it," she said. Then she turned over and unhitched the back of her bikini top again.

Oh, man, Eric thought. *You're killing me.*

One minute she was totally digging him, the next she was pushing him away. What was her problem?

SIX

Grip with legs, lift arms, grip with hands, and climb! Grip with legs, lift arms, grip with hands, and climb! Nathan felt like a caterpillar as he shimmied up the palm tree, but it was a huge relief just to hang on. With his feet tied around the trunk, he didn't have to worry about falling off every two seconds, but that didn't make the climb any easier.

He glanced down and saw Daley gnawing on her lower lip. She looked really worried. Maybe she *would* be upset if he fell down. Or maybe she would just miss having him to boss around. He was exhausted, and his brain was weary from trying to figure out the whole tree-climbing trick. He wasn't thinking anymore. He was on autopilot.

Nathan kept the coconuts in view. *Eye on the prize!* Besides, it wasn't any fun to look down.

"You okay?" Daley shouted from below.

Nathan's voice was a croak as he answered, "N-n-no

problem." He made a mistake and let his eyes wander downward. He was only about halfway up the tree, but it looked like half a mile to the ground. Truth was, he wasn't all that big on heights. Lex and Daley were whispering to each other. Probably making bets on whether he would make it or not.

I don't care what they think—I'm not going down without taking some coconuts with me! Being able to stop to rest— that was the best part of this new system. But he had to keep moving. If he started sitting there for too long, he'd get scared and probably give up. Plus, if you didn't keep moving, bugs were liable to get on you. That's what had killed him last time. This humongous spider had crawled up his arm and freaked him out a little bit. He'd only fallen off because he was trying to knock the spider off his arm.

He inched upward some more.

Sweat dribbled down his cheek and dropped off his chin. Daley must have noticed his exhaustion. "I'll get you some water," she called. "You're gonna need it."

Nathan nodded numbly. What he needed was an extra pair of hands.

"Hang on tight!" Lex called.

"Thanks!" Nathan rasped. "I hadn't thought of that."

With a grunt, he gripped the trunk with his arms and lifted his legs higher, scraping them painfully against the rough bark. *Eye on the prize . . . eye on the prize . . .*

When Daley reached the fire pit, she was a bit surprised to find Eric doing the boiling, filtering, and pouring. Melissa staggered out of the jungle with a full water jug in each hand, and looked as if she could barely take another step.

Melissa dropped onto a towel and sat there, panting.

"You're doing great," Eric said cheerfully. "I can probably take over for you . . . eventually."

Melissa sighed loudly, but she looked too tired to talk.

Daley said, "I need water for Nathan. He's building up a huge sweat doing nothing." She rolled her eyes for good measure.

"The good water's over there," Melissa answered, pointing to a crate of filled containers.

Daley picked up a bottle just as Jackson stormed up to the fire pit. She smiled at him encouragingly. "Hey, any—"

With a growl, Jackson stuck his fishing pole into the fire and marched off.

"—Bites?" Daley said, finishing her sentence.

Eric chuckled. "It doesn't matter how many of those he makes, huh? He's got more chance of catching a fish in that fire than in the water."

Melissa reached into the flames and rescued the fishing pole, and the two girls looked worriedly at each other. *No point asking if we're having fish for dinner,* Daley thought. It was as if all the boys were self-destructing. Or at least spinning their wheels. Was Eric even really hurt? No matter—she couldn't dwell now.

Time to go back to see if Nathan is still alive, Daley thought.

What am I doing wrong?

Jackson shuffled wearily back to the boys' tent, determined to get some well-deserved rest after all his failure. Even fishing in the tide pools and inlets, using bait and hooks, he had failed to catch a single fish. Not to mention most of the tide pools had been about the size of his finger. The inlets seemed a little more promising—but by the time he'd tried one of them, he had pretty much lost all hope. It had seemed pointless toward the end—the fish were laughing at him. The girls would be laughing at him, too, but it was hard to laugh on an empty stomach.

He crawled into the tent and went straight to his sleeping bag. Before he lay down, he thought he would look for another plastic container with his name on it. Sure enough, there it was. Jackson rushed to the doorway, hoping he could spot his mysterious "friend." As usual, his friend had left no clues.

Why should I listen to someone who sneaks around and won't even show himself? Why doesn't he go fishing if he's so freakin' smart? Jackson wanted to throw the box away, but he was just too hungry and too frustrated to quit. He ripped open the box and found what looked like the remains of a pearl necklace, plus more hooks and a colorful coral sinker. He quickly read the note:

"Fish like shiny things. Use all the hooks and something to weigh it down. Stay low; they can see you. A friend." Yellow paper, red pen.

This isn't funny anymore. It never really was. Jackson wanted to throw the note away and crawl into his sleeping bag, but he knew instinctively that the advice was good. He shook his head and staggered to his feet. *Somebody is trying to help me. That's a good thing. It's probably Lex . . . or Daley. Whoever it is, his or her intentions are right.*

Okay, "friend"—I'll give it one more shot.

Almost there! Eye on the prize . . . eye on the prize . . .

Nathan's arms and legs ached, and blood dripped from his skinned ankles. Another lunge ... another few inches closer to the prize. The wind blew, causing a pleasant rustle in the palm fronds, but he *hated* the wind. He could feel the palm tree swaying with every gust, and it was a sickening feeling—like being stuck at the top of a Ferris wheel in a storm. Only, *that* was safe compared to this foolish stunt.

Now I know how King Kong felt at the top of the Empire State Building. Y'know ... just before he died.

Nathan didn't dare look down, because the ground, Daley, and Lex all seemed like a mirage. The only reality was the incredible height he had climbed, plus the coconuts. They were closer than ever ... just a few feet above his head. If he reached out, he could almost touch them! But he couldn't reach out, because he needed both hands to hold on to the rough tree trunk.

If I fall from this height, I won't be getting up again.

Nathan was so tired and sore that he could barely move another inch, but he had to keep going. After coming this far, he had to finish the job. The giant coconuts glinted in the sun, and they looked like they were ready to tumble down at the slightest touch. A rush of adrenaline pushed Nathan the last few inches, and the coconuts were within his reach ...

Only he couldn't let go of the trunk.

"You're there!" Lex shouted from the distant earth. "You got it!"

"N-now what?" Nathan croaked.

"Pull tight with your legs and use your hands," Lex answered. "You won't fall."

Nathan gulped. "Well, that's easy for you to say ... from way down there."

Lex just shrugged and gave him a goofy smile.

I've done the hard part, Nathan told himself. *All I have to do is let go with one hand and take a swat at those stupid coconuts.*

He pulled himself together and gripped the trunk as tightly as he could with both legs and one arm. His first lunge at a coconut missed, and so did his second. He gasped, feeling himself slipping, but he shimmied a few inches higher and tried to get a better angle.

"I . . . don't . . . even . . . like . . . coconuts," he muttered through clenched teeth. Frustration spurred him on, and he let go with one hand and lunged again for the nearest coconut. He whacked it hard, and the giant fruit fell from the tree and dropped to the ground like a bomb.

"Yes!" Nathan cried triumphantly. A flood of enthusiasm rushed through him. He'd done it! All along he'd known. He'd just *known* it was possible. And now he'd done it.

Daley rushed into the clearing and picked up the huge coconut. She looked at Nathan in amazement. "He did it," she said in complete disbelief.

"Awesome!" Lex shouted. "Keep going!"

Having gotten one coconut, Nathan set his sights on the whole bunch of them. With a hard swat, he hit the branch and knocked a major clump of coconuts into the air. They plummeted to the ground, narrowly missing bonking him on the head. He scooted around a few inches toward the other side of the tree as Daley scooped up the cluster.

"He did it again!" she said joyfully.

"Look out below!" he yelled. Then he knocked another coconut free. It fell to the ground with a satisfying thump. He reached out for another one, felt his grip slip. Whoa! He gripped the tree fiercely. Okay, this was getting a little scary again.

After the initial surge of energy, he felt his strength fading. He looked down at the ground, started counting. One, two, three—then he stopped. Okay, whatever. Surely he'd gotten a couple or three coconuts for each kid. That ought to hold them for tonight. After all, they still had a few more rations left.

We won't go hungry tonight, Nathan thought with pride. One of Nathan's ancestors, Nathaniel Edmund McHugh, had been a famous explorer. The whole time he'd been here, Nathan felt like he was trying to live up to the reputation of his namesake. And for the first time he felt like maybe he was making a little progress in that direction. *Okay*, he thought. *Let's quit while we're ahead.* He shimmied down the tree as fast as he could. With gravity helping him, it didn't take very long to get down. He was never more grateful to touch the ground in his entire life.

He felt himself grinning from ear to ear. So were Lex and Daley. "That was pretty cool," Lex said.

Nathan brushed pieces of bark and leaves off his hands and clothes. He ignored all his scrapes and bruises. "No problem," he said. "Just doing my part. How many did I get?"

Lex did a quick count and answered, "Six."

"Not bad. I'll do better next time," Nathan promised. "Let's get these back to the others." He could hardly wait to see their faces.

"I'll get the rest," Daley said with a sly smile. Carrying the coconuts, she and Lex walked across the clearing into the jungle.

"Rest? What rest?" Nathan asked, trailing after them.

Daley smiled. "While you were climbing, we took turns looking for other fruit."

"Really? How'd you do?"

Daley pushed back a fern to reveal a treasure trove of fruit. There were bananas, figs, papayas, mangoes, and stuff Nathan didn't even recognize. Now he felt like he had fallen out of the tree . . . onto his head.

"The coconuts are good, too," she assured him.

The first few minutes of spearfishing had been fun. But after that, it had pretty much just been work. But now Jackson was so tired that effort was pretty much out of the question. The fish would come to him or they wouldn't. Either way, he wasn't gonna knock himself out.

He had found a beautiful, secluded little inlet about half a mile down from the camp. A little outcropping of strange black rock stuck up at the edge of the water, making a natural seat. Jackson plunked down on the rock. It was warm from the sun.

Odd, twisted trees with knobby roots that stuck up from the water surrounded the small inlet. He looked down into the clear water, spotted a few small fish moving around in and out of the tree roots. If there were small ones down there, maybe there'd be some that were big enough to eat.

Wearily, he pulled out the little bag of leeches, threaded one onto a hook. He carefully assembled the hooks, sinkers, and the pearl necklace lure all at the end of one line. He even used an old plastic bottle as a bobber. This contraption looked kind of crazy. But at this point, what did he have to lose?

He kissed his lures for good luck, swung his pole back, and cast the line into the sparkling water. The bottle bobbed on the surface, just like it was supposed to. The "friend" had said fish liked shiny things. He positioned the lure so that it caught a ray of sunshine down in the middle of a dark tangle of roots. Then he secured his fishing pole in the rocky ground and sat down to wait.

This has to work, he decided. *We're starving, and my "friend" has to be fresh out of tips.*

Eric could see Taylor skulking across the beach. *What an amateur*, he thought, still pretending to be asleep. *Who does she think she's dealing with?*

His hand tightened around the full squirt bottle he had hidden down his shirt. He waited until she was in range. Then he jumped to his feet and let her have it. Taylor squealed with alarm and shot a weak stream of water at him, which missed. "Psyche!" he shouted.

"I hate you!" Taylor yelled, shrinking back from the deluge.

He dashed after her, squirting away . . . crashing straight into Melissa.

Where did she come from?

Eric had that sickening feeling of a criminal caught red-handed. And Melissa was his judge, jury, and executioner.

Melissa's normally friendly face cracked into a mixture of disbelief and anger as she tossed her water bottles onto the sand. Eric gulped and tried to explain, but she shoved him hard in the chest. He managed to stay on his feet, but he wilted under her fiery gaze.

Fuming, Melissa strode off. He thought about running after her. But what could he say after being busted so badly? He didn't know what his punishment would be, but he guessed that his job of boiling water was over. Even Taylor looked shocked at this unexpected turn of events.

Who knew Melissa could ever get so mad?

SEVEN

Jackson had known his grandfather for a few years when he was a kid—back before everything had started going wrong in his life. Back before his father left. Back before his mom started having all her problems. Jackson's grandfather had grown up way out in the country in Mississippi and was always talking about how he used to go fishing all the time when he was a kid.

"Best thing in the world, fishing. You just lie back and let the hook do the work," his grandfather always said. "The only work involved is staring up at the sky and thinking great thoughts."

For the first few minutes after he'd thrown the hook into the water, Jackson had kept jerking on it and moving it around and peering at it. But finally he just got tired. The late afternoon sun had begun to warm him finally. And the worry and nervousness had started to float away.

Jackson looked around him. Everything was strange and

beautiful and lush. Back in L.A. you had to practically pass an act of Congress to make anything grow. L.A., after all, was a desert. Here, everything was lush and green. Large, fragrant flowers were growing everywhere, bees were flying around, strange brightly colored birds flitted by occasionally.

Something about it calmed his nerves, and suddenly he realized he was falling asleep. He hadn't slept worth a hoot for three days. Truthfully? This felt pretty great. After a while he stopped caring about fish. To heck with it. They'd bite or they wouldn't. Like his grandfather said, "Lie back and let the hook do the work."

He jammed his pole into a crevice in the rock next to his leg, and leaned back. Within seconds, he started to doze.

Just as the world had begun to fade pleasantly away, someone started thumping on his leg.

"Go away," he said. "I'm sleeping."

The thumping continued.

"Cut it out!"

Still, the irritating thumping continued. He opened one eye to see who it was. There was no one there.

Then he realized. It was the pole, jiggling against his leg. He sat up straight.

Yes! Something down in the water was pulling on his line! He grabbed the pole and began to pull back.

What a lazy, sleazy, scamming jerk! Melissa was still seething with anger as she boiled and filtered the drinking water. Eric was supposed to be hauling water again, but she doubted he could be trusted to do that anymore. She bet he was in the plane, taking a nap. It took all of her restraint to not hunt him down and beat him to a pulp.

Maybe lugging water all day from the well is hard work—maybe we should have rotated our tasks—but that doesn't excuse faking an injury. Eric is the lowest of the low—lower than the leech that I just picked off my leg!

At the very least, she should tell Jackson and Daley about Eric's fake-out. They would come up with a good punishment for him, but what could they do to make him work? They couldn't cut him off from food, because there wasn't any food to speak of. It seemed as if all of them were already being punished.

Melissa heard singing, or cheering, coming from the jungle. She whirled around in time to see Daley and Lex emerge from the jungle, hauling a big blue sling between them. Her ears perked up when she made out the words of their happy chant:

"We have bananas, hey! We have papayas, hey! We have some figgies, hey! We have coconuts, hey!"

Nathan trailed behind them, his arms loaded with coconuts. Melissa jumped to her feet and waited expectantly until the foragers dumped their bounty onto a towel near the fire. Fruit had never looked more fresh, more delicious, or more exciting.

"We come bearing gifts from the benevolent spirits of the jungle, with a message," Daley declared.

Melissa giggled and asked, "What's the message?"

"It's . . . 'Let's eat!' " Lex shouted.

Suddenly Eric ran out of the jungle, hauling his water like a good boy. He dropped the jugs and fell to his knees in front of the bounty of fruit. "Yes!" he yelled as he picked up a juicy mango. "This is like . . . like . . . a tropical Thanksgiving! I take back everything I said about you guys. Most of it, anyway."

Taylor showed up moments later. When she looked at all

the food, she wrinkled her nose and said, "Um, we're gonna get really sick from eating nothing but fruit."

"Not a problem," said a weary male voice.

They all turned around to see Jackson carrying a string of six fat fish. Now the cheers really went up, and the camp rocked with thoughts of happiness and full stomachs.

"Yeah! You did it! All right!" they shouted at once.

Taylor still wasn't happy. "Yeah, woo-hoo," she said with a frown. "Who's gonna clean those things? Not me. I'll puke."

Everyone else cringed, too, at the idea of cleaning fish. The one who looked most disgusted was Eric, which gave Melissa an idea. *Let the punishment fit the crime.* If he ever wanted forgiveness, this was his chance.

"It's all taken care of," Melissa said with a grin.

"It is?" Daley asked doubtfully.

"Yeah," Mel answered. "Eric was just telling me that he *loves* cleaning fish guts." She punched him in the ribs meaningfully.

"He did?" Lex asked with disbelief.

"This Eric?" Daley pointed to the goof-off.

"This Eric?" Eric echoed.

Melissa narrowed her eyes at the water boy. "Yeah! Unless you've suddenly got some kind of injury that's gonna stop you from doing it that you want to tell everyone about. Hmm?"

Eric looked around the group, then back at Melissa, and gulped squeamishly. "Uh, no. I'm cool . . . I can do it."

The group shouted their encouragement and slapped Eric on the back. For a moment, he did look okay with it . . . until Jackson shoved the biggest of the fish into his face.

It was hard to tell who looked more miserable, Eric or the fish.

Banana peels, plates, water bottles, and fish bones lay scattered all around the beach. And there were no moms there to make the kids pick them up. Of course, nobody could move because they were so stuffed. Daley had told everyone to eat as much as they wanted—tomorrow there would be rationing, but not tonight.

Tonight it was a tropical Thanksgiving, like Eric had said. Daley slumped back on her towel, feeling pretty good about their chances of survival . . . now that they knew how to coax some food from this island.

Eric lay in the sand, groaning. "This is just . . . sick." He let out a huge belch that echoed around the campfire, and Taylor gave him a disgusted look. Then the petite blonde let out a burp that was even louder, and everyone laughed.

Daley sighed with contentment. "I hate fish. I hate bananas. I'm not even sure what a fig is, but this was the best meal I've ever had." Everyone groaned their agreement.

Eric sat up, still looking hungry. "What about the coconuts, Chief?" he asked, looking at Jackson.

Jackson was struggling to saw through the tough outer husk with their biggest kitchen knife, but he wasn't getting very far. He looked as if he needed an ax for the job.

"Working on it," Jackson said breathlessly.

Daley sat up and looked around the camp for Nathan, who was the only one not sitting with the rest of them. He sat on a piece of wreckage twenty feet away, slowly finishing his meal. Nathan looked sick, too, but not because he was too full.

I'll talk to him, Daley thought. *Don't want him to zone out on us. We need everybody to make it through this.*

She walked over to Nathan and sat beside him. "I guess you're feeling pretty dumb," she remarked.

"Gee, don't sugarcoat it," he muttered.

"What can I say? I told you that you didn't have to do it."

"Yeah, well, whatever."

Daley shook her head in amazement. "I gotta say, though ... that was pretty brave. No way I could have done it." She set a banana on his plate and walked away. A glance over her shoulder revealed that Nathan was smiling at the peace offering.

That felt good, Daley thought. *Maybe ... just maybe ... if we live long enough, we'll be able to work together.*

Jackson had dug the knife so far into the coconut husk that he couldn't move it anymore, so he just banged the coconut on a rock. Finally it split. "Yes!" he shouted.

But there was another nut inside, like one of those crazy nested dolls from Russia. This one had a thinner shell, and when he shook it, he could hear the coconut milk splashing around inside.

"You gotta crack it open," Lex said, looking over his shoulder. "I'll work on it." The kid picked up the coconut and started to walk away.

"Hey," Jackson called, and Lex stopped. "Thanks."

The boy looked curiously at him. "I haven't done it yet."

"You know," Jackson said softly. "A friend." Lex just stared blankly at him, and Jackson went on, "The stuff in the tent? The boxes, the notes?"

"Huh?" Lex cocked his head, frowned.

Jackson studied him. Lex had his usual expression of open curiosity on his face. There didn't seem to be any trickery there, anything hidden.

"Never mind," Jackson said.

EIGHT

Daley

Okay, we've got enough food for a few days, and we're learning how to get more. Water is no problem, as long as the people collecting it don't kill each other. We've got shelter and firewood, although we use a lot of wood to boil the water. We've got plenty of sunshine—I know that from my sunburn.

We're still missing a few basic necessities ... like clean clothes. But now we've got enough water to do laundry.

The main thing that's bothering me right now is my sunburn. God, it's killing me! I'm slathering on the sunblock all day, but I guess I'm just too fair-skinned to be standing around in this bright sun all the time. But there's not much I can do about it.

And anyway, things could be a lot worse.

It was their fourth day on the island. For the first time since they'd crashed, Daley was starting to feel like maybe this wouldn't turn out to be a total disaster. She was trying to document the changes in their little camp, to use the camera to show that they'd started pulling together as a team.

Daley picked up the camera and panned along her clothesline, which was full of garments and stretched the length of the plane. While she was shooting video, she scanned the rest of the camp and caught everybody working.

Jackson was cutting firewood.

Nathan was cracking open his precious coconuts.

Melissa was tending her fire.

Lex was doing something with the emergency signal kit. She had no idea what.

Eric was hauling water. Or at least he was supposed to be.

And Taylor was ... napping on the wing of the plane. With a scowl, Daley set the video camera back on the ground.

Daley

We've more or less settled into a routine. Meaning some of us do more, and some of us do less. Some of us do a lot less. I'm not complaining ... much.

She turned off the camera and went back to wringing wet clothes in a makeshift bucket. It was boring, grueling work, but it felt so good to put on clean clothes. There was another thing they could all use, but she didn't know how to bring up the subject. It was kind of delicate.

A shadow fell over Daley, and she looked up to see Taylor holding up one of her many bathing suits.

"This is fuchsia," the blond girl explained. "Be careful. I don't want it coming back faded pink." She set her skimpy suit on top of the pile, then sailed back to her beach towel.

Daley's mouth dropped open. She looked around—everybody else was still working, all except for Taylor. She had returned to her usual position . . . flat on her back and sound asleep.

That was the last straw for Daley. She grabbed the bathing suit, marched over to Taylor, and threw it in her face. "Get up," Daley snapped.

Taylor looked at the bathing suit and said, "Wow, that was fast."

"This is not a spa," Daley said. "I am not your staff."

Taylor gave her a little wave. "Oh, could you slide over a smidge? You're blocking my sun."

"Yeah, sure," Daley answered from force of habit. She started to move, then got mad all over again. "Stop! We're trying to survive here, Taylor! What don't you get about that?"

Hearing the dispute, the other kids crowded around, staring.

"What's going on?" Lex asked.

"Nothing," Daley snapped. "That's the problem. We're working our butts off, and Taylor's kicking back like she's at Venice Beach."

Taylor wrinkled her nose. "Oh, please! Nobody goes to Venice Beach."

"Ugh! Can she be any more clueless?" Daley flapped her arms in frustration.

Nathan smiled. "Absolutely. You'd be amazed."

"Well, I've had it," Daley declared. "If she won't do her fair share of the work, then she won't get her fair share of the food and water."

That sunk in, and Taylor jumped to her feet. "What? I'll, like . . . *die!*"

"Then make yourself useful," Daley said before she stormed off. The others quickly fled, too, leaving Taylor all alone to fume.

No guilt, Daley thought. *No backing down. That twerp knows she has to pull her own weight.*

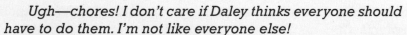

Ugh—chores! I don't care if Daley thinks everyone should have to do them. I'm not like everyone else!

Taylor crossed her arms and stamped her foot in the sand. Eric stumbled out of the plane, surprising her.

"Some of us are trying to sleep, you know," he murmured, yawning.

Taylor crossed her arms and scowled. "If Daley wants trouble, she has come to the wrong place!"

Eric yawned and said, "You mean she's come to the right place. If you're gonna give her trouble, then she's come to the *right* place."

"Oh. Right. That's exactly what I mean." Her lips set in a pout, Taylor turned and stalked off.

⬩

With the food problem under control for the moment, Nathan was looking around for something else to do. People could only eat so many coconuts.

Okay, I've been spinning my wheels a little bit, but none of us are survival experts. I just gotta find the right niche and show everyone how valuable I am. Especially Daley—she needs to know that she can count on me. I can be a go-to guy.

He was walking along the tree line when he spotted Jackson dragging a large branch down the path. Nathan hurried up to him and said, "Hey, let me give you a hand."

"It's okay, I got it," Jackson answered, panting from exertion.

Nathan saw the camp knife stuck in the ground, and he grabbed it. "I'll start cutting it up."

Jackson reached for the handle and took the big knife away from him. He acted like he was afraid Nathan was going to hurt himself. "It's cool," Jackson said. "I'll handle the knife."

He dragged the big limb toward camp, leaving Nathan feeling lower than low. *Hasn't anybody in this crew ever heard of teamwork? How can we survive if we can't trust and respect one another? Obviously Jackson thinks I'm useless.*

Other people must need my help, Nathan decided, and he marched off to find them.

⬩

Owww! Fire on the deck! What's up with this stupid sunburn? Daley winced as Melissa put a gob of lotion on her roasted shoulders. She had come to the fire pit to get more water for washing clothes, and she figured she would get some first aid, too. Melissa normally had a gentle touch, but it didn't feel very gentle today. *And I really need some TLC.*

"This is bad," Melissa said softly. "You should stay out of the sun, and wear a shirt."

Daley gave a hollow laugh. "Stay out of the sun?" She motioned at the wide swathe of beach. It wasn't like there was a lot of room to get out of the sun. "Yeah, right. Besides, it hurts too much to wear a shirt. I'll deal."

Taylor staggered out of the jungle carrying one bottle of water. With great effort, she dragged it to the pit and set it among the other bottles.

"Are you happy?" she asked Daley, a note of challenge in her voice. "I'm gonna take a break . . . if that's okay with you."

"Yeah, whatever."

Taylor smiled coolly and said, "Thank you oh-so-very much." She shuffled off, massaging her shoulder.

"At least you got her to do a little something," Melissa said.

Daley pointed to all the bottles. "Well, I have to admit, that's more than a little. That's a lot of water."

Melissa sighed and answered, "Uh . . . I got most of that."

"Really? How much did Taylor get?"

"Including the bottle she just dropped off?" Melissa asked.

"Yeah."

"The bottle she just dropped off," Melissa said.

Daley bolted upright, anger surging through her body and flaming as hot as her sunburn. She sputtered when she asked, "You . . . she . . . it took her *three hours* to get one bottle?"

Melissa shrugged, and Daley jumped to her feet, totally livid. *This is not the prom decorating committee or cheerleading practice—this is survival! In regular life, maybe you get a pass just because you're cute and blond, but regular life ended when our plane crashed.*

Daley started to run after Taylor, but halfway across the beach she saw Jackson chopping wood. She changed direction and charged up to him.

"We are in a life-or-death situation," she told Jackson. "There's no telling when we're gonna get rescued, so if we don't all work together and do our share then . . . then . . . we could die. Okay, I said it. We could *die*."

Jackson shrugged, like *Thanks for the news flash.* "Yeah, so?"

"So do you see what Taylor is doing?"

He shook his head. "No."

"Exactly!" Daley shouted. "Because she's doing nothing. Nothing! We give her food and water, and we clean her clothes and give her shelter. I feel like her mother, and I don't even *like* her."

Jackson just kept right on cutting his branch. Annoying.

"Jackson, you're the leader," she told him. "Lead!"

Jackson sank the knife into the branch with a loud smack. He paused, wiped his brow on his sleeve, and—for the first time—actually looked at her. "Okay," he said, "I got a plan."

She paused, leaned forward. "Yeah?"

"As leader, I'm giving *you* the job to do something about it."

"Me? Why should I be the one to—" She stopped to think about it for a moment and decided that this was a rare opportunity to whip the prom queen into shape. "Really? You're giving *me* the job to get Taylor to work?"

"Congratulations. You've been promoted."

"And you'll back me up," she asked, "with anything I say?"

"Yeah."

Oh, she is so mine, Daley thought.

NINE

Nathan had wandered back and forth on the fruit trail twice without finding even a rotten fig. He hadn't found any firewood, either. He had the gloomy feeling that he was just pacing, working off nervous energy. *There's so much I could be doing, if the others would just give me a chance to prove myself.*

When Nathan got back to the beach, he spotted Melissa trying to fix the poles on the canopy over the fire pit. *Here we go!*

"Hey, Mel," he said, grabbing the pole from her hands. "Why don't you take a break? I'll finish this."

"Uh, that's okay," Melissa said quickly. "I already took a break and uh . . . maybe Jackson needs help."

"Oh, no, he doesn't," Nathan answered. "I already checked with him."

Melissa grabbed the pole back from him and started wrestling with the canopy in earnest. "That's okay, thanks anyway."

Glumly, Nathan backed off. *Fine, then.* There wasn't much else to do but make a video diary. A few moments later, he was sitting in front of the camera with the tape rolling. He wanted to be upbeat and positive, but he wasn't exactly feeling that way.

Nathan

I'm starting to get the vibe that people think I'm useless. Okay, maybe I was spinning my wheels getting the fire going the first day. And my solar still and water catchers were pretty lame. I did fall out of that tree and nearly killed myself. And I didn't think to look for fruit that was lying right on the ground before climbing up in the first place.

Wow. Maybe I am useless. But I'm not. Really! I gotta turn this around.

Ticked off, Taylor took a slow walk through the trees. The last person she expected to find was Eric, napping under a tree.

He's doing less work than I am, she decided, *but nobody is ragging on him for it!*

Taylor marched up to Eric, put her hands on her hips, and said, "Unbelievable."

Immediately he rolled over and began doing sit-ups. "Forty-six . . . forty-seven . . . forty-eight."

"What are you doing?" Taylor asked with disgust.

"Trying to keep in top shape," he panted, "so I can do my fair share of the work."

She rolled her eyes. "That's just ridiculous."

Eric dropped to the ground, exhausted after three sit-ups. "Yeah, really," he answered, "but it sounds good."

"Why is Daley giving me such grief?" Taylor asked, flapping her arms. "I mean, look at you. You're totally worthless, and nobody bothers you."

"That's because I know human nature," he answered smugly. "It's all about perception."

"English, please. This isn't school."

Eric looked around and said, "Don't fight them. Make them think you're doing it their way just once, and they'll back off. Then you can do whatever you want."

Taylor drummed her fingers on the trunk of the palm tree Eric had been lying next to, thinking about what he had said. She noticed that one of her nails was chipped. That was really not good. She was going to have to fix that.

"Hm," she said finally. "You know, the thing is, Daley's right. There really is a lot of work to be done here."

Eric stared at her.

She held out her finger. "I mean, look at this. At home I would have just gone to the salon to fix my nails. Now I'm gonna have to do it myself."

Eric raised one eyebrow. "Yeah."

Taylor looked around. "I wonder if there's anything on this island I could use to wax my legs with."

Eric lay back down. "Wake me up if you find the solution to that one."

One thing was for sure. If she was going to have time to keep her nails in shape, she was definitely going to have to find a way to avoid all this silly stuff like carrying water.

Taylor

It's perfect! I can do what I want to do, as long as I *look* like I'm doing what Daley wants me to do. I'm not really sure how to do that. But I'm going to. Do that, I mean . . . what Daley wants. Or thinks she wants. Or I want. Or something like that. It's perfect.

Lex is always keeping busy, Nathan thought as he strolled through the jungle. *And he's just a little kid. Nobody hassles him and treats him like a total loser, like they do me. I'll see if Daley's bro needs some help with heavy lifting or soldering . . . or something.*

So he hunted Lex down in the shade of the wrecked DeHavilland, where he was messing with some stuff from the plane's survival kit. There was a case full of cool orange guns, orange sticks, and other objects Nathan didn't recognize.

"What's all this?" Nathan asked eagerly.

"It's awesome," Lex answered. "Emergency signal gear from the plane. There are flare guns and there's a whistle and—"

Nathan grabbed one of the orange flare guns.

Lex looked horrified. "Whoa, careful," he warned. Lex took the device and carefully put it back in the case. Then he held up several strips of orange and black nylon fabric, plus some metal struts. "Check this out, Nathan."

"What is it?" Nathan asked.

"A signal kite," Lex said. "We can fly it up over the trees and let it sail there 24-7. Somebody ought to spot it."

Nathan grinned. "That is so cool!" He snatched the kite

out of the boy's hands. "I can build this."

"Uh, I can too," Lex said nervously.

"No problem," Nathan insisted. "I've made loads of kites."

Lex didn't look too happy about giving up his fancy signal kite, but Nathan didn't care. He was certain he could build a kite better and faster than some ten-year-old. The kite was a great idea, and he wondered why they hadn't put it up earlier.

Well, that's because I wasn't in charge of it, he decided. *I'm going to get us rescued . . . and have fun doing it!*

Daley was on a mission as she strode across the beach, the camp shovel gripped firmly in her hand. If Taylor thought she could hide from her, she was badly mistaken.

She spotted Eric lying under a tree, doing sit-ups. "Forty-five . . . forty-six . . . forty-seven," he counted.

That sight was odd enough to make her stop for a second to ask, "Why are you doing sit-ups?"

He stopped to answer breathlessly, "To keep in top shape, so I can do my share of the work."

Daley rolled her eyes. Who did he think he was kidding? "Where's Taylor?"

"No clue." He craned his neck to look at her back. "Hey, you should stay out of the sun—that's a nasty burn."

Daley nodded distractedly. She looked around and spotted the girls' tent. She marched over there, with Eric following cautiously behind her. The tent flap was closed, but Taylor's fashionable boots were outside drying in the sun.

Daley shouted, "Taylor? I want to talk to you."

There was no answer, and Daley stamped her foot in the sand. "I know you're in there. Your boots are right here."

"I'm busy," came an annoyed voice.

Daley's lips thinned in anger. "Doing what?"

"Sit-ups."

Daley glanced at Eric. "Sit-ups? Why?"

"Well, duh!" came the answer. "So I can get in top shape, so I can do my share of the work. Two . . . three . . . four—"

Daley narrowed her gaze at Eric, who shrugged innocently.

"Would you please come out?" Daley said sweetly. "I have something for you."

Taylor instantly popped out of the tent, rubbing her eyes as if she'd been napping, not exercising. "Really?" she asked happily. "What is it?"

Daley pushed the shovel into her hands, and Taylor looked at the tool as if it were a snake. "How thoughtful," she said snidely.

"We need a latrine," Daley declared, "and you need to dig it."

Taylor's eyes widened. "Dig? Please, I could hardly be expected to do that."

"Really?" Daley said with bogus innocence. "And why might that be?"

Taylor held out her hand, extended her middle finger.

"Oh, that's really mature," Daley said.

"No! Seriously! Look!"

"At what?"

"Duh! My nail."

Daley examined Taylor's pink-painted fingernail. Did she have an infected hangnail or something? "It looks fine to me."

Taylor stared at her. "It's chipped," she said finally. "It's totally chipped. These nails cost three hundred dollars, and now they're ruined."

"So take five minutes and file it . . ." Daley said. ". . . *after* you dig the latrine." She jammed the shovel into the sand and started walking away.

"Um . . . Daley?" Taylor called after her.

Daley stopped, turned around. "*What*, Taylor?"

"Um . . ." Taylor blinked. "What exactly is a latrine? Is it some kind of mushroom?"

"No," Daley said, speaking very slowly so that Taylor could have a chance to understand each and every word. "A latrine is a big, deep trench that you're going to dig far enough away from the camp—downwind—so that we don't have to worry about bacteria getting near the food or water to make us sick. Once it's done, it'll be a safe place that we can all use . . . to go to the bathroom."

It took a moment for Daley's words to sink in. But when they did, Taylor's eyes widened in alarm, and she cut loose with a long, blood-curdling scream.

At the fire pit, Jackson heard the horrible shriek and stopped pouring water to look at Melissa. The dark-haired girl shrugged, and they both looked around, wondering if a shark or a wild boar had attacked somebody. When Jackson saw Taylor charging toward him, with Daley right behind her, his shoulders slumped. It was worse than a shark, he realized.

Don't tell me those two are fighting again! I thought Daley could handle this by herself. Oh, why didn't I go off with Captain Russell and the others to explore the island?

Taylor stomped up to Jackson and said, "I won't do it. I just . . . won't!"

"What?"

"Daley has no business bossing me around," she ranted. "My own *mother* doesn't make me do chores. That's why they make maids."

Melissa made a big show of looking around. "Gee, Taylor," she said, "I'm not seeing a maid anywhere."

Jackson was a little surprised. It wasn't like Melissa to be sarcastic. But apparently after her experience with Eric the day before, she was getting as fed up with the Eric and Taylor Show as everybody else.

Before Taylor could respond, Daley charged up and tried to hand her a shovel. Taylor backed away from the shovel. "Jackson," Daley said, "you put me in charge of getting Taylor to do some work."

"Look," Taylor said, "I am not going to dig a . . . a . . . poopy pit!"

Jackson tried not to laugh, because this was serious business. They actually did need a latrine, but he had hoped someone would *volunteer* to dig it. They continued to fight over the shovel, with Daley foisting it on Taylor, who refused to touch it.

Finally Daley declared, "We need a latrine. You need to work. It's the perfect solution."

"There is nothing perfect about it," Taylor answered. "You can't make me."

"I can."

"You can't."

The two faced each other silently for a minute. Taylor turned to Jackson. "Look at this! Look at my nail! They'll get totally wrecked if I have to do a bunch of . . . *digging*." She said the word like it was the worst thing a human being could possibly do.

Jackson just looked at her. He was kind of interested to

see how Daley would work this out.

"Besides . . ."—Taylor's face softened and she gave Jackson a big-eyed look—". . . this is a job for somebody strong and muscular and manly. Someone like . . . you, maybe."

Jackson felt the corner of his mouth turn upward in a half smile. Pretty hilarious. "Daley?" he said. "Thoughts?"

Daley paced for a moment, then calmly said, "Okay, Taylor. Here's the plan. If there's no latrine by supper, then your rations will be cut in half. No latrine by tomorrow, they'll be cut in half again, and again the next day, and again the next day. Until you start pulling your weight."

Taylor kept looking at Jackson with her wounded puppy expression. "Jackson?"

Daley also looked coolly at him. "You said you'd back me up."

Jackson took a deep breath and looked at Melissa, who couldn't do anything but give him an encouraging smile. *Yes, I'm the leader. Yes, I gave Daley control over Taylor, which seems really stupid now. I hate this.*

"Taylor, just do some work. Okay?" he told her.

She screamed again, tossed the shovel onto the sand, and stalked off. Daley picked up the shovel and charged after her, telling her how and where she was supposed to dig this wonderful latrine. For a moment Jackson felt bad about bossing Taylor around.

But only for a moment.

TEN

A s luck would have it, Taylor marched into the jungle and finally stopped at a very good place to dig the latrine. It was away from everything and had some tall ferns in the area . . . for privacy.

"Are you still following me?" Taylor snapped.

Daley ignored her. "Let's see . . ." She used the shovel to draw an outline in the dirt. "Right here, Taylor. Four feet long, a couple of feet wide, and at least two feet deep."

Taylor clamped her mouth shut and looked at the outline on the ground. Finally she said, "That's not a trench, that's a canal. How am I supposed to do that?"

"Come on," Daley said, "this isn't rocket science. Here, I've got something else for you."

Taylor rolled her eyes. "No thanks, I didn't think much of your last present."

"Wear my shirt," Daley said, untying it from around her waist. "Trust me, you don't want to get a sunburn."

With two fingers, Taylor took the shirt as if it were full of cooties. Daley also took a scarf out of her pocket and asked, "Do you want a bandanna for your hair?"

"A bandanna?" Taylor sneered. "That's so seventies, and not even the cool retro kind."

"Fine," Daley said as she handed the shovel to Taylor. "Finish this by dinner, or there won't be any dinner . . . for you."

"I thought you said *half* rations," Taylor said. "I'd still get half my dinner."

"Well, see, you ate half of your daily rations for breakfast today. That means you're done eating for the day." Daley tossed the shovel into the middle of the rectangle she'd drawn on the ground. "Unless, of course, you finish digging."

Taylor still stood there holding Daley's shirt between two fingers. There wasn't anything left to say, so Daley turned to leave.

"Ugh," Taylor said. "Khaki."

Nathan sat in the shadow of the wrecked plane with all the parts of the signal kite spread out before him. It was kind of a mind-bender how it all went together. Lex jumped out of the passenger cabin and tried to stick a sheet of paper in his face.

"I've got the instructions," Lex said.

Nathan waved him off. "We don't need them; this is cake."

"Nathan, we gotta do it right."

"We will," Nathan assured him. "No problem."

He picked up a strut and managed to slide it into some narrow loops in the nylon fabric. *There, that looks about right.*

Lex gave a loud sigh and climbed back into the airplane.

At the fire pit, Melissa poured some boiled and filtered water into a drinking bottle. Behind her, she heard rustling in the jungle, and she turned to see Jackson hauling two full water jugs toward the fire. He was the only one strong enough to carry two of the big plastic bottles when they were filled to the brim. She tried not to stare at the muscles in his arms as he set the jugs on the ground.

Melissa wanted so badly to tell him . . . a million things. She would probably never have the courage to tell him she kind of . . . sort of . . . had a little crush on him. But romance wasn't something any of them needed right now, when survival was taking up every moment of the day. Maybe if they ever got rescued and things returned to normal, she could finally tell him how she felt.

No, probably not. Melissa had never gotten too bold with boys before, and she wasn't likely to start now.

But she could give him a compliment. Even boys liked compliments. After he set the bottles by the fire, she said, "I think you did the right thing with Daley and Taylor."

"Yeah?" His tone was doubtful.

"Sure. There was a problem; now there isn't. And we get a latrine." She smiled at him.

"We'll see," Jackson said. He went to the pile of firewood and began breaking the branches into smaller pieces. For some reason, he could never stand still long enough to hold a conversation.

"I knew you'd make a good leader," Melissa added.

Jackson looked sort of embarrassed. For a second she almost thought he was going to smile at her. But then, instead, he frowned like he'd thought of something he needed to do, and charged off to another task.

Melissa felt like crawling into the latrine, whenever it was ready.

I guess all those dance lessons and cheerleading and shopping trips were a waste of time, Taylor thought as she struggled to dig in the hard ground. *I should've been in a chain gang in prison, preparing for my new role as a manual laborer.*

"Ouch!" she cried as she broke another fingernail. Despite digging like a gopher for hours, she was only about halfway done. And she was sweating like a . . . boy! When she used Daley's ugly shirt to wipe the sweat off her brow, she felt something in the pocket.

Taylor opened the flap and took out a family photo of Daley with her mom and dad and Lex. *Oh, how utterly sweet. Barf.*

She caught sight of something moving behind a nearby tree trunk. How very sneaky.

"Hey! Lame-o!" she shouted at Eric. "What are you doing?"

"This may shock you," he said, "but I happen to be unoccupied for the moment."

"No duh," she snapped. "Come help me!"

"I can't do that," he told her.

"Because?"

Slowly Eric got up, stretched his arms, and strolled toward her. "Because if I helped," he explained, "you wouldn't appreciate the lesson you're getting here."

"Oh, really?" she answered with a scowl.

Eric took off his straw hat and sat on a fallen tree near the edge of the latrine. "Taylor, Taylor, Taylor," he began, "you're learning that there's beauty in defeat."

"I am?"

"Absolutely. You're going to find that defeat presents you with a unique opportunity."

"Opportunity for what?" she asked doubtfully.

Eric smiled slyly and said, "Well, for revenge."

Taylor cocked her head and considered his words. *Yes, he does have a point.* She looked again at the photo of Daley and her family, then touched the collar of Daley's shirt.

For the first time that hot, miserable afternoon, Taylor smiled.

ELEVEN

Lex didn't want to hurt Nathan's feelings, but he was really worried about the signal kite. It could make the difference between being rescued or turning into the Swiss Family Robinson, stuck there indefinitely. They might get only one chance to contact the outside world, and that kite could be it. They didn't have anything else that would work 24-7. Lex tried to tell himself that Nathan was smart, a good student, and he must have flown kites when he was a kid.

He'll do okay.

As an experienced kid brother, Lex was used to dealing with Daley and her friends, but that was back in real life, not life-or-death survival time. He worried that the older kids might look down on him, but so far they had been cool. He wasn't in competition with them, and that was also good. Still, they were a long way from becoming the team they would have to be if they hoped to survive—for weeks, maybe even months.

"Hey!" called a voice.

Lex looked up and saw Nathan marching toward him, grinning and carrying something that *looked* like a kite. *If it doesn't work, let him down easy*, Lex told himself.

"I told you I could do it," Nathan said, holding out the orange-and-black box kite.

Lex inspected the contraption and nodded. "It is pretty cool." He didn't say how relieved he was.

Nathan grabbed the kite and handed Lex the spool of string. "I'll launch it. Keep up the tension."

Grinning, Nathan ran north along the beach.

Unfortunately, the wind was directed toward his back.

"Wait!" Lex called. "That's not the right—"

He clammed up. *I have to be careful what I say to him*, Lex thought. *Nathan is the kind of guy who has to make a mistake before he can learn from it.*

Before they could launch the kite, Melissa and Jackson walked up and stood beside Lex.

Nathan shouted, "Get ready!"

Lex shrugged and let the line play out.

"Shouldn't he be going the other way?" Melissa whispered.

"Yes," Lex said. He waited for Melissa or Jackson to tell Nathan, but nobody said anything.

Still grinning, Nathan stood by the shore and held the kite high in the air. "Ready?" he called. "One . . . two . . . three!"

He let go of the kite, and it plunged right into the sand. Lex gulped, hoping the kite wasn't badly damaged.

"Did it break?" Lex called.

Nathan quickly scooped up the kite, gave everybody a thumbs-up. "Only a flesh wound!" he said cheerily.

He backed up about thirty feet, then ran toward the

water again, releasing it as he reached top speed.

Again, it flipped and smashed straight into the sand.

Nathan looked at it irritably. Trotted back, started to run again.

"How soon before he breaks it?" Jackson said.

Lex didn't say anything. This was not good at all.

Nathan released the kite a third time. This time the kite plastered itself to his body, the stiff wind pressing it against him. He went leaping around, arms waving wildly until finally the kite slipped off of him and catapulted into the surf where a wave smashed it into the sand.

"Hold this," Lex said, handing the string to Melissa. Then he ran toward Nathan. "Is it broken?" he called.

"*Yeah*, it's busted," Nathan yelled, fishing the kite out of the surf. Water poured off the orange cloth. "It totally won't fly."

Lex grabbed the kite, inspected it quickly. Miraculously it wasn't broken.

"It's not broken," Lex answered patiently. "You gotta launch into the wind—with the wind facing you."

Nathan frowned and picked up the kite. He jogged past Lex and the others on his way down the beach. "I knew that," he said. Melissa and Jackson smiled their encouragement, but Lex could see the worry on their faces.

Now facing the wind, Nathan held up the kite. This time, Lex gripped the spool tightly, because he was pretty sure it was going to take off. *If it's been put together right and isn't damaged.*

"Ready? Do it!" Lex shouted.

Nathan let go of the kite and it sailed straight up into the sky. Everyone cheered, but Nathan cheered the loudest. Lex walked backward, making the string even tauter, and the kite gained altitude. *No doubt about it—we're in business!*

But before their cheers had even died out, the kite wheeled, spun, dove toward the ground, smashed into the sand again.

"Uh-oh," Lex said. "It's not supposed to do that."

He ran toward the kite again. Nathan was there first, however. He picked it up and this time it hung limply in his hand. One of the spars lay on the sand.

"Maybe I'd better go back and look at the directions," Nathan said.

"Here, I'll help," Lex said, stooping to pick up the spar.

Nathan grabbed it before he got the chance. "I got it," he said sharply.

"I don't mind. I'd be happy to—"

"I said, I *got* it," Nathan said.

Lex watched him as he walked away toward the boys' tent, the wet string trailing behind him on the sand.

"Not so great with the kites, huh?" a voice said. Lex turned and saw Taylor watching Nathan disappear into the jungle.

"Aren't you supposed to be digging the latrine?" Daley said sharply.

Taylor smiled airily. "I don't know *what* you're talking about."

Nathan had felt so defeated that he just left the kite inside the tent. He had glanced momentarily at the instructions. But they must have been written by somebody in China or someplace, because they made zero sense.

He wandered out to the coconut trees, thought about climbing up to get some more. But when he looked way up at the swaying fronds, he just didn't have the energy. Then he walked down the beach to the inlet where Jackson had caught all the fish yesterday. But since he didn't have a pole, there wasn't any way for him to fish.

Six coconuts. That had been his sole contribution to this whole expedition. Was there something wrong with him? Was he just unlucky? It was hard to figure.

He kicked the sand angrily. Wouldn't you know it, there was a big shell buried just beneath the sand. He stubbed his toe, a wave of pain shooting up his leg. He picked up a stick and smashed it against a tree. That felt a little better.

Finally he gave up on finding anything to do, figuring he'd just go back, take a little nap. Maybe after a decent nap, his confidence would return.

He unzipped the flap of the tent, started to lie down on his bed. Then he noticed something sitting on top of the kite. A small plastic box with his name written on it in red magic marker. He picked it up and opened it.

Inside was a note written on a piece of yellow paper that had been folded into a small square, and a piece of thin red fabric.

The note was written in block letters with a red felt-tip pen: "This type of kite needs weight for stability. If you knot this piece of fabric a couple of times and then tie it to the small metal eye in the base of the kite, it will fly perfectly."

The note was signed:

"A friend."

"Huh," Nathan said. "Weird." For a minute he thought about burying the note—along with the box—in the little bag of trash they'd hung from the ceiling of the tent, and then going to sleep.

But at the last minute, he decided to try what the note said. As he tied the bright piece of fabric onto the tail of the kite, he wondered who the "friend" was. Probably Lex.

He'd kind of snapped at the kid after the kite had crashed. Lex was probably trying to be tactful and make Nathan feel better. Which was nice of him. But still, it made him feel a little stupid, having to take advice on kite-flying from a ten-year-old kid.

Taylor sat in the shade and watched Eric dig. Even though he was sneaky and lazy, she did have one piece of leverage over him. He was totally hot for her. It hadn't taken her long at all to get him to dig the hole for her.

Sweat was streaming from his face. "Why do I keep getting stuck with all the digging?" he said. "You know I practically dug the whole well, too?"

"I heard you dug the last spadeful and Daley did the rest of it," Taylor said.

"Yeah, well, Daley *would* say that, wouldn't she?" Eric threw down the shovel. "This blows chunks."

"Want some water?" Taylor asked.

He smiled gratefully. "That'd be great, thanks."

"Yeah," she said. "It's back at the camp. Help yourself."

Eric looked at her blankly. "You're not gonna get it for me?"

She smiled pleasantly. "Wasn't really planning to."

Eric glowered at her, climbed out of the hole, and walked off toward the plane. "Feel free to break a sweat while I'm out of your way," he said over his shoulder.

She waited until he was gone before she stood up and looked at the hole. The problem with getting Eric to do the digging for her was that he did really sloppy work. The whole thing was liable to cave in the way he was doing it. She sighed, grabbed the shovel, started fixing his shoddy work. Every few minutes, she paused to listen. It would not be cool for him to show up suddenly and see her working. He'd feel much better about the whole thing if he thought he'd done it all himself.

"Here," Nathan said, "let's try again."

"What's that?" Melissa said.

"It's a tail," Nathan said. "This kind of kite won't fly properly without one. For some reason it was missing from the kit."

"Oh," she said. "That's pretty fabric. What's it made out of? It looks like you tore it off a girl's dress or something."

"Uh ..." Nathan said. "Yeah, it's ... uh ... from one of Captain Russell's Hawaiian shirts."

"Hey, good thinking!" Melissa said. "That's very smart."

Nathan smiled, hoping he didn't look too sheepish. Now that she mentioned it, it was kind of girly-looking fabric. Sheer, silky stuff. He wondered where the fabric *had* come from. He hoped Lex hadn't raided somebody's luggage for the strip of cloth.

Lex watched expressionlessly from a spot over near the plane. Not wanting the kid to think he was hogging all the credit, Nathan gave him a conspiratorial wink. Lex frowned curiously back at him.

Well, whatever. If he wanted to keep his contribution anonymous, that was fine with Nathan.

"All right," Nathan said. "Let's try this again." He pulled the kite slowly across the sand, letting Melissa pay out the string.

He licked one finger, held it up in the air. Supposedly that helped you tell which direction the wind was blowing. He'd never really seen what the point of that was, though. Anyway, it was pretty obvious which way the wind was blowing. He held the kite up, felt it tugged vigorously in the wind.

Yeah! This was gonna be it.

He ran up the beach into the wind. The kite immediately responded, practically leaping into the air. It didn't feel all nervous and jittery like it had before. Just a steady, firm tug. He let go and the kite leaped upward, climbing straight up in the steady wind.

Everyone watched nervously. But this time there was no sign of a crash. He took the spool of line from Melissa, let it spin rapidly. The kite climbed and climbed.

He turned to the onlookers and said modestly, "Well, I think we did it this time."

Melissa gave Lex a joyous hug. "It's like having a permanent distress signal in the sky!" she said.

Nathan clapped his hands together, feeling a burst of pride and enthusiasm. "That's exactly what I figured," he told Melissa. "This baby can fly 24-7."

Lex frowned slightly. Nathan realized belatedly that he had stolen the line from Lex.

"Good work, Lex." Nathan clapped him on the shoulder. "We did it together, huh?"

Lex shrugged. "You pretty much did it all."

Nathan smiled. "Hey, it'll be our little secret."

"Huh?" Lex said.

Nathan ruffled Lex's hair. Odd kid. Smart, but odd.

From the fire pit, Daley gazed at the kite flying over the beach and smiled. And it was hard to smile with prickly raw pain stretching across her back. Mostly she winced. *Yeah, everyone thinks it's so great to be a redhead.*

Daley couldn't stand to wear a shirt, but she couldn't go

out in the sun without one. She could wear sunscreen, but she didn't think her ravaged skin could stand another minute of sun, screened or not. Shade and this lotion brought the only relief, and they were both temporary.

I don't want to turn into a vampire, but I could do my share of the work at night. Then I'd sleep all day and be just like Taylor and Eric. That would be annoying, but something else worried her much more.

What if this is only the beginning of our ailments? There are all sorts of nasty tropical diseases we could get that would make this sunburn seem like a pimple. We've got to get out of here before dysentery, malaria, or injuries slam us hard. If we are all sick at once, the water and food will disappear fast.

We just have to get out of here.

She heard footsteps and turned around to see Taylor and Eric headed her way. When Taylor tossed the shovel onto the ground, Daley was certain she was in for a fight.

But Taylor just gave her a superior smile and said, "Done."

"It's a thing of beauty," Eric added, "and open for business . . . so to speak."

"Seriously?" Daley asked, not bothering to hide her surprise.

"Check it out," Taylor said. "Better yet, you can be the first to use it. I'm going swimming." She and Eric headed off toward the surf.

Knowing these two, Daley suspected some kind of trick, but she couldn't say anything until she actually did check it out. Melissa, Jackson, and Lex joined her as she walked into the jungle, and the three of them reached the latrine a couple of minutes later.

And it really was a latrine! The trench was deep and wide, just like the dimensions she had laid out. The walls were nice and square. It looked totally shipshape. Jackson nodded, impressed, and Lex jumped down into the pit.

"Cool!" Lex said.

"It's . . . perfect," Daley added. "I'm stunned."

Melissa frowned in thought. "How do we use it? I mean, well, you know what I mean."

"I can make something to sit on," Lex answered as he climbed out. "We just gotta make sure that afterward we toss a little sand in to cover up, you know—"

"Right," Melissa said, wrinkling her nose. "Gross."

Jackson looked at Daley and said, "Taylor did well."

Daley nodded, unable to argue with that.

"I think I'll be the first one to break it in," Jackson said, leaping into the latrine.

The others said their good-byes and beat a hasty retreat. Daley had to admit that she probably owed Taylor some kind words, maybe even an apology. She hadn't actually expected the princess to get the job done. *Taylor must really want to keep eating.*

Taylor and Eric floated in the ocean on the plane's life preservers, grinning and splashing around. Taylor couldn't remember when the warm, salty water ever felt so good. *Revenge really is sweet!*

"That was so fun," she told Eric. It would be delicious to see how this played out. The gruesome discovery. The horror. The tears.

"See?" he asked. "And now she'll think twice before messing with you again."

Taylor nodded thoughtfully. *I had no choice. I was driven to it!* And she didn't feel one bit guilty. She waited until Eric turned away, then she splashed him, nailing him in the side of the face.

"Hey!" he spluttered. Then he grinned and came after her, doing his best to splash her back.

"Too slow!" she taunted. Then she nailed him again.

Lex concentrated hard while he tied the last joint on his makeshift latrine seat, which used the real toilet seat from the plane and lots of wood. He was working so hard that he didn't see someone sneaking up on him until Nathan jumped from behind the plane and pointed a flare gun at him.

"Freeze!" Nathan shouted, sounding like he was on a SWAT team.

Lex screamed in alarm and ducked behind his chair. He didn't want a flare down his throat.

Nathan laughed out loud and pointed the gun upward. "Dude, relax," he said. "It's empty."

"Don't mess around like that," Lex said angrily.

"You're right. I'm sorry." Still laughing, Nathan helped Lex to his feet and brushed off his pants. Then he noticed the latrine seat. "Hey, is this good to go?"

"Yeah," Lex answered, who was still kind of mad.

"Awesome," Nathan said. He grabbed the seat and rushed off toward the jungle.

"Be careful!" Lex yelled. "Don't use poison-ivy leaves to . . . you know."

Nathan chuckled and waved back. "Thanks, I'll remember that!"

Very carefully, Lex picked up the flare gun and returned it to the case. Unfortunately, he had to keep one of the guns loaded, in case they had to use it at a moment's notice.

Sitting in the shade of the plane, Taylor looked with horror at the bumps all over her hands. "Eric!" she said with alarm. "Look! I've got a tropical disease! My hands are breaking out in hideous boils."

Eric blanched for a moment, but he worked up his courage and took a look. When he smiled, she didn't feel relieved at all. "How'd you get all those blisters?" he said. "I didn't see you doing any digging."

"Blisters?" she said.

"I was wondering," he said. "Every time I took a break, the hole seemed to get bigger." He examined her palm. "You'll live."

"Oh, thanks for all the concern and everything!"

He abruptly changed his tune. He began to massage her palms. "Now soak these hands in clean water. We'll get you some ointment and give you a nice rubdown—"

Bingo, Taylor thought, realizing the cause of Eric's change of heart.

Daley passed by, looking concerned. "Oh, hi," Eric said. "Just doing a little first aid. Her hands are pretty torn up."

"Whoa," Daley said when she looked more closely. "Yeah, they are." The redhead actually winced, which made Taylor feel a little better. She had almost started to feel guilty, but the blisters were enough to help her keep focused on her anger.

"I'll live," Taylor said coldly. "Even though my nails are wrecked."

Biting her lip, Daley sat beside them on the beach towel. "Look, Taylor," she began, "this is no excuse, but I've been in a nasty mood because of this sunburn. And . . . I was wrong.

I shouldn't have gone off on you like that. I'm sorry."

"Really?" Taylor was a little shocked. Daley was overdosing on self-righteousness pills.

"Yeah, and you did a great job on that pit," Daley said. "Seriously. I feel so bad I made you do it all on your own. It looks better than I would ever have hoped."

"Oh, um, wow," Taylor answered. "I didn't think you'd actually apologize."

Daley smiled. "Yeah, well, I'm really not a jerk. How about if I make it up to you? How about if I finish your laundry? I promise not to fade your suit, and I'll dry it in the shade. Fuchsia, right?"

Eric cleared his throat and looked away, and Taylor jumped to her feet. This wasn't working out the way she had expected. Nice, apologetic Daley was never in the plans—Taylor was used to mean, overbearing Daley.

Nervously, Taylor said, "Right. You know, I'm gonna be the first one to use that latrine."

"Too late," said Daley with a laugh. "Everybody's using it."

"Everybody? Already?" Taylor was stunned. Somehow imagining what would happen was a lot better than it actually happening.

"It's so gross," Daley answered. "But it's perfect. You did really well."

Eric stood up abruptly and started to slip away. "I, uh, I got some stuff I gotta, you know, check on." In a flash, he was gone.

"Eric?" Taylor pleaded, but he had already deserted her. *Crud. What am I going to do?*

Daley frowned and asked, "What's going on? You look kind of funny."

The air between the two girls froze. Everything seemed

to spin all around Taylor. *Maybe I just made an enemy for life.*

Taylor cringed. "Well, you said it yourself . . . you were being kind of a jerk. So you really kind of deserved it."

"Deserved what?" Daley narrowed her eyes.

"You know that shirt you lent me?"

"Yeah?"

From the other side of the plane, Lex yelled with alarm, "It's not a toy, Nathan!"

"I know that!" Nathan answered. "It's not loaded."

"What about my shirt?" Daley asked.

Taylor managed a pained smile and said, "Well, when I finished digging the latrine . . . I . . . sort of left it at the bottom . . . under some sand."

Daley stared at her with disbelief, which quickly turned to anger. She started shoving the smaller girl backward. "You left *my* shirt at the bottom of the latrine? That everybody's been using?"

"Oops!" Taylor said sheepishly.

Daley stalked her through the sand at the same time that Lex was yelling angrily at Nathan. It was all sensory overload, and Taylor just wanted to get away . . . far away.

"I want my shirt back now," Daley ordered.

"What!" Taylor asked in alarm. "Eww, no way."

Taylor tried to run for it, but Daley cut her off. "Taylor, you dig it up, or I promise I will make your life miserable."

"I . . . I thought you said you weren't a jerk?"

"I lied!"

Daley rounded the tail of the plane at the same moment that Nathan did, and the two of them collided. A rocket exploded from Nathan's hand as he fell to the sand, and a bright flare soared through the sky.

For a moment everybody froze, watching the bright

red ball of fire shoot into the air, a thin trail of smoke rising behind it.

"Uh-oh," Nathan said.

"No," Daley said. "It's not gonna . . ."

The flare was heading straight toward the orange kite.

"No, it couldn't . . ." Nathan said.

But it did.

For a moment it appeared the flare would miss the kite. But it hit the tail, snagging in the red fabric, and then flipping wildly in the air. Fire shot out all around it, showering the kite with sparks.

And then the kite erupted in a ball of flame.

Everyone stared in shock as the kite burned brightly, then imploded, the nylon fabric shrinking into a tattered black ball as it burned. The remains of the kite began to fall, bits of flaming cloth dripping off into the air like molten fire. The kite fell and fell, finally hitting the sand near the waterline, a hundred yards down the beach.

It lay there, smoldering.

Nathan looked glumly at the flare gun in his hand. Melissa and Jackson frantically grabbed water bottles, ran toward the burning kite, and tried to put out the fire. But it was too late. There was nothing left but a gooey black mess.

They both looked up accusingly at Nathan. Nathan dropped the flare gun on the sand and buried his face in his hands.

TWELVE

Nathan wondered if he should ask Taylor to dig him a hole to crawl into. *No, she already has enough blisters.* He didn't know what Daley was doing when she ran into him, but he couldn't blame her for the accident. Melissa and Lex tried to put the singed kite back together, but he could tell it would never fly again.

I've really mangled things this time, Nathan thought. *Might as well bite the bullet, though.* He walked over to Jackson and said, "There were two flare guns. One wasn't loaded."

"I guess that would have been the other one, huh?" Jackson asked.

"Yeah." Nathan looked down at his shoes.

Jackson shrugged his shoulders and said, "It's okay. It's done. Nobody really got hurt." He turned to Nathan and added, "Do us all a favor and stop trying so hard, all right?"

Nathan gulped and nodded. Was it wrong to want to help? To want to be involved? Did they want to be a community?

A family? Or a bunch of strangers who hardly spoke to one another?

Nathan

There hasn't been a single thing I've done since the crash that has turned out right. All I want to do is be useful. But I'm starting to think they'd all be better off . . . if I wasn't here.

I trusted her with my shirt. Stupid! My picture of my family, my last stick of gum, my only decent shirt. How could I be so dumb?

As the sun went down that day, Daley was back at her makeshift bucket, washing clothes. Survival seemed a lot harder when they were all fighting with one another and doing stupid things . . . things that could be prevented. Food, water, shelter—that wasn't all there was to survival. Getting along was a big part, too. *Getting revenge should never be part of the plan, even though I want to strangle Taylor.*

Daley was still fuming when Taylor approached. She was about to get up and move when Taylor said, "Just so you know, I'm not totally heartless. Before I buried your shirt, I took this out."

Taylor handed Daley the photo of her family, the one she always carried in her shirt pocket. Daley gaped in amazement at the picture—relief spilled over her. She was still furious, but she managed a grateful smile. "Thanks."

Taylor stuck around to help her hang clothes on the line.

They didn't talk at all and barely looked at each other, but they were working together nonetheless.

Afterward, Daley took a few minutes off from washing to talk to the video camera.

Daley

I admit it, I always put people into easy categories. Friendly, unfriendly, smart, dumb, annoying, not annoying. After losing my shirt to the ick, I have to admit it isn't always that simple. People have more than one side. Good and bad. Including me.

She turned off the camera and found Nathan looking at her. He was the one person on the island who looked more miserable than she did. Daley picked up her bottle of lotion and touched her raw back. Tomorrow she would really have to stay out of the sun, even if it meant slacking on her chores.

"At least the sun's going down," she told Nathan. "My burn can't get any worse."

Nathan peered at her back and shook his head. "That's not a sunburn."

"What?"

"You're covered in red splotches," he answered. "I've seen that before. It's some kind of allergic reaction. Are you putting stuff on it?"

"This after-sun lotion." She showed him the bottle.

"You know, I bet if you stop using that stuff, it will clear right up."

Daley blinked in amazement. She'd wondered why it was

only getting worse the more she put on. "If you're right . . ." Daley hesitated. "Well . . . I *so* owe you."

That brought a tired smile to Nathan's face. "Happy to help."

As the sun dipped into the satin sea, Daley hoped that maybe all of them were a little closer to that one intangible thing they needed to survive: respect.

We all have faults, we all have tempers, and we all have grudges. But all we have are each other.

THIRTEEN

Jackson didn't know if he was getting better as a fisherman, but he did have less trouble with tangled lines and snagged lures. He was able to fish for hours and not get his gear into a knotted ball of string. But he worried about what they would do when they ran out of earrings. There weren't too many other things lying around that he could use for gear.

He could see Lex scampering through the tide pools and rocks, exploring the inlet. Lex was always up to something surprising—and surprisingly helpful.

Suddenly Lex slipped. "Owww!" he yelled, dropping out of sight.

Jackson tossed his pole away and whirled around.

"Jackson!" Lex yelled. "Jackson, c'mere, quick!"

Jackson jogged as fast as he could over the rocks and sand to reach Lex. His biggest fear was someone getting hurt out here in the middle of nowhere—with no doctors, no clinics, not even a drugstore. "You all right?" he shouted.

Lex scrambled onto the rocks and waved both arms. "You gotta see what I found!"

Jackson walked gingerly over the sharp and uneven rocks around the tide pools until he finally reached the boy. He peered into the murky water where Lex kept pointing, but he didn't see a darn thing.

"I was walking along and tripped over it," Lex said excitedly. "It was total luck."

Jackson nodded, still not understanding. Lex reached into the sandy depth and pulled out something that looked like a small black rock with white flecks. He proudly showed it to Jackson and exclaimed, "Can you believe it?"

"Uh, sure. Nice rock," Jackson answered.

"It's not a rock!" Lex exclaimed. He banged it on a boulder until it split open. The inside was hollow and oozed a gooey white substance. "It's a clam, or an oyster—I don't know which. But it's food!"

Jackson poked at the gushy meat, still unimpressed. "Not a whole lot there to split seven ways."

Lex laughed and plunged his hands back into the tide pool. He came up juggling a dozen of the mollusks. "Good thing there's about eight thousand more where that came from!"

Now Jackson grinned. This would be a lot easier than catching fish. The hard part would be convincing everyone to chow down.

Melissa set the video camera on its tripod and looked around the jungle. She was well off the beaten track—the one that ran between the well and the fire pit—because she wanted to record her video journal in private. They were all being good about taping their video diaries and not rewinding to watch the others. Melissa sure hoped it would stay that way.

With a sigh, Mel turned on the camera and squirmed nervously.

Melissa

Good morning, uh, diary. This is Melissa. Obviously. We've been stranded almost a week, and nobody talks much about getting rescued. Because . . . well, we don't know why it hasn't happened. It's scary. What's going on?

Melissa took a deep breath.

Are they looking in the wrong place? And if they don't find us right away, are they gonna think—

She didn't finish her grim thought.

Panic doesn't help. These videos are about documenting what we're going through, so there's something I want to say. I think the main reason we're doing okay . . . is Jackson. He's really being strong. He doesn't talk much. He doesn't have to. Everybody sees how he does the most work. And doesn't complain or get emotional over stuff. He's not hard to look at, either.

He hasn't been at school long, so nobody really knows him. But he seems, I don't know, troubled. He's gotta open up someday, and when he does, I hope it's with me. I guess it's obvious I like him, but I'd never tell him. No way. That would make things too weird. But when we get off this island, I'm going to let him know how I feel . . . and hope he doesn't laugh.

Eric waited patiently behind the bush. Or tree. Or whatever it was. The huge leaves of the plant he was hiding behind covered him up nicely, with just one little gap that he could peep through and watch Melissa's entire embarrassing performance. He had to struggle not to laugh. She'd kill him if she knew he was listening in.

He'd seen her creeping off with the camera a few minutes ago, trying to look all innocent and everything. But Melissa couldn't hide anything. It was all right there on her face. She was obviously having some "deep thoughts" that she needed to get off her chest. He had been pretty sure she was going off to spill all the intimate juicy stuff to the camera. So he'd followed.

And of course he'd been right. He wasn't sure how he'd be able to use the knowledge he'd just acquired. But it would come in handy eventually. *Knowledge is power, baby. Even here.*

No . . . especially *here.*

When Melissa finished her video diary, she headed straight back to the beach.

Eric waited a couple of minutes, then took the long way through the jungle—to make it look as if he'd been hauling water. That's when he spotted Nathan carrying an armload of fruit. Nathan was walking in this weird way. Sort of hobbling and bowlegged. It was pretty goofy-looking.

Eric jogged up to him and said, "What's with you, cowboy? Been in the saddle too long?"

Nathan gulped and looked around. When he was satisfied that nobody could hear them, he whispered, "I got a rash."

"A rash?" Eric asked. "What kind of—"

"Shhh! Jeez!" Nathan cautioned, still looking around. "I think I got it from wearing wet shorts."

"Ouch." Eric winced.

"Yeah, my legs are on fire. It's all down the insides and—"

"Please, thank you," Eric said, signaling him to shut up. "Too much information."

Nathan's eyes widened in horror, as if he just realized who he was talking to. "Don't tell anybody, all right? It's kind of, uh—"

"Say no more, dude. It goes to my grave." Eric held up three fingers. "Scout's honor."

"I didn't know you were a Scout."

"I'm not." Just seeing all the food Nathan was carrying made Eric's mouth water. "Here, let me help you carry some fruit."

"Man," Nathan said wearily, "that'd be great."

Eric took one banana from the pile in Nathan's arms and walked off, peeling it.

"Great, thanks," Nathan called after him. "Sure appreciate the help!"

Hey, nothing to it, bro. It wasn't even lunchtime and he'd already found out about a pathetic teenage crush and an embarrassing rash. How could he use this treasure trove of embarrassment? He'd think of something.

He tossed the banana peel on the ground next to the trail and smiled. It was going to be a great day, he could tell already.

Since the plane crash, Taylor figured she had suffered more than anyone. Her fingernails were absolutely ruined now. Hideous. And . . . *blisters?* Taylor Hagan with *blisters?* Something was massively wrong with this picture. And people were totally not treating her the way she was used to. Back home, she had been practically queen of the universe. The head cheerleader, most popular girl, everybody said she was the best-looking girl in the school. Not to mention rich. She'd never done a chore in her life.

But here, none of that mattered. Jackson ignored her. Nathan was so absorbed in his own little drama that he barely looked at her. Lex thought she was an idiot. Daley had threatened to starve her. And Eric—this total nobody who she wouldn't have even talked to back at school—was starting to act like he thought he was her boyfriend or something. Yeah, right. That'd be the day. Sure, he could be fun sometimes. But he was chasing her around all day, trying to squirt her. Which was funny, like, once. But the joke had worn thin a long time ago.

And if I think about the food we have to eat, starvation is beginning to sound good! And does anyone even thank me for keeping the batteries charged? Nuh-uh.

At least she had her speaker wire back, because Jackson

was fishing with the line from the burned-up kite. All that was trivial compared to this new indignity. Taylor couldn't believe what the boys had brought back to camp this time.

"You want us to eat rocks?" she asked.

"No, no, they're oysters!" Daley said excitedly, picking one up. Jackson grabbed another and began to mutilate it with the cooking knife, making Taylor cringe.

"And there's a ton of them!" Lex claimed.

"This is incredible," Daley gushed. "Lex, you found a whole food supply!" They rapped knuckles.

Against her better judgment, Taylor watched Jackson trying to open one of the oysters. Without warning, he cracked it open and showed her the slimy contents of the grimy shell.

"No way," she said, gagging. "That's like eating boogers."

"How would you know?" Daley asked.

Taylor gave Daley a withering look. But as usual, Daley didn't seem to care. Back in L.A., Taylor had made girls *cry* just by looking at them like that. Here? People just laughed at her.

Melissa poked one oyster dubiously with her finger. "Are they safe?"

"I think so," Lex answered.

"You *think*?" Taylor said, rolling her eyes. "*Poison* boogers. Oh, this just keeps getting better and better."

"There might be toxins," he admitted, "but I think that's kinda rare. And this is about survival."

"It's true," Nathan said. "At home, no way. Here, I'm hungry. I'm sure it'll be just fine, you know."

Eric gestured at the oyster. "Then go ahead, bro."

Nathan eyed the shell uneasily. "Uh . . ."

Eric snickered.

"Okay, look, guys, I've got an idea," Melissa broke in. "Maybe one of us should test one."

Eric looked around the group. "Then what? If that person doesn't die a horrible, puking death, we chow?"

"Guys . . ." Daley started, using what Taylor had come to think of as her Voice of Doom tone. "We're gonna run out of dry food soon, and we don't always catch fish."

"It's not a big risk," Lex insisted, "and we don't get enough protein from fruit."

Eric stared at the boy genius. "Really? I guess we've been reading up on our three food groups, huh?"

"Actually it's five," Lex said, missing Eric's sarcasm.

"Oh, gee whillickers, thank you for that correction," Eric said.

"Shut up, Eric," Daley said. "Look, bottom line, we gotta try it."

The silence was deafening. No one was hungry—or crazy—enough to eat the toxic booger.

"Don't everybody volunteer at once," Eric said with a laugh.

"We draw sticks," Jackson said. "Does that sound fair to everyone?"

They nodded solemnly. Taylor searched desperately for a reason why she shouldn't be included, but she came up dry. She thought about trying to concoct some kind of shellfish allergy or something, but by the time she came up with a plausible story, Jackson had already broken up a bunch of twigs from the woodpile and arranged them in his hand. The tops were even, and the bottoms hidden. "Short stick eats," he said, holding the bunch out to Eric.

Eric pulled a twig from Jackson's fingers, and it looked medium-sized to Taylor. "Is this long or short?" Eric asked.

Melissa was next in line, and she quickly grabbed one

that was the same length as Eric's. "It's long!" she gushed with relief.

"Yes!" Eric shouted, dancing with joy. "My string of unbroken luck continues to roll onward today."

"What other lucky things have happened to you today?" Melissa said.

"Oh, nothing, nothing," Eric said nervously.

Nathan wiped his hands apprehensively on his shirt before he took a stick. But his matched the others. More celebration: He punched at the air like he'd just scored a touchdown. *Well, my odds are going down the toilet*, Taylor thought.

It was almost a relief by the time Jackson got to her and offered her the four remaining twigs. She grabbed one and looked at it.

Of course. Just my luck.

"Psyche!" Eric shouted.

"No way," Taylor declared. "I am not eating toxic snot."

Daley glared at her. "That was the deal."

Lex picked up the oyster Jackson had opened and held it out to Taylor. It glistened moistly in the harsh sunlight, little bits of icky, disgusting blobs floating in the wet surface of the—

Suddenly she jerked backward. "It *moved!*" she shrieked. "I saw it move!"

"Sure," Lex said. "Technically, they're still alive."

"Oh, my God!" Taylor wrinkled her nose. "What do I look like? A cannibal?"

Lex said, "Um, actually cannibalism means eating a member of your own—"

Taylor held up one hand, stuck her palm in Lex's face. "Forget it. I'm not going to eat 'em anyway, so—"

Impatiently, Jackson grabbed the oyster and poured the

meat down his throat. Everybody made a face and fell silent, slightly awed and slightly grossed-out. Jackson looked thoughtful, but the group couldn't tell what he was thinking.

"Whoa," Eric said, impressed.

Jackson turned to Lex. "How long till we know?"

"A couple of hours, I guess," he replied.

Jackson nodded. And burped.

FOURTEEN

Eric trudged along, groaning under the weight of the water jugs he toted. One of the jugs slipped from his clammy hand, and he had to stop to retrieve it. As the day grew hotter, the water jugs grew heavier and more slippery. The leeches grew bigger, the cups got smaller, and dirt caked everything he touched. Eric really hated hauling water from the well.

Nobody's job was worse than his, he decided. He wondered how the others could pull such a guilt trip on him. But who could he appeal to?

Melissa.

He waited until she walked back to check on him.

"Hey, what's up?" she called.

"I need a favor," he said bluntly.

"Sure, what?"

Eric slid next to her, just in case the trees had ears. "I want to dump this water-fetching job on somebody else."

Melissa's smile faded, and she said, "We've all got jobs, Eric."

"Well, I'm over this one. Could you tell Jackson to give me something a little less, I don't know . . . like work?"

She sighed and answered, "Tell him yourself. He doesn't listen to me."

"He might," Eric whispered, "if he knew how much you *like* him."

Melissa's mouth dropped open. "I . . . I don't like Jackson."

"Oh, really?" Eric asked. "I thought you wanted him to 'open up to you, because he's so troubled' and—"

"You looked at my video!" she snapped at him, flushed.

"I did not!" he answered. "But I just kind of happened to be in the neighborhood when you were taping. I can't help it if I overheard a little of what you were saying when you were making it—"

Now Melissa went into full panic mode. "No! That is so wrong!"

"Yet so true." He stepped away from her, certain that he had her where he wanted her.

"Eric, you can't say anything," Melissa begged him.

"I don't know," he answered thoughtfully. "Like you say, it's important we're all honest with one another and share our—"

"*Anything!* I'll do anything for you to keep quiet," she promised.

Eric gave her a sympathetic smile. "You know what?" he said. "I think maybe we can work something out."

Perfect.

An hour later, after Melissa had carried three full bottles back to the fire, boiled and poured and filtered, and stumbled back to the well, she had fire in her eyes. This was *twice* that Eric had manipulated her into doing his work. She spotted Eric lounging under a tree, eating a banana, and scowled at him.

"Don't hate the player, baby," he said. "Hate the game." He motioned to the four new bottles he had ready for her. Well at least he was doing *something*. Filling a few bottles was not exactly challenging work. But it was better than nothing. "Anyway, Melissa, I'm doing my part. You know what they say about me. Good ol' Eric—he's all about teamwork."

She moved the bottles over to the far side of the fire. So he'd at least have to stand up to get to them. "It's more like: Good ol' Eric—he's all about blackmail."

He put a look of bogus indignation on his face. "I wouldn't call it that. I'd call it . . . uh . . ." He scratched his head for a moment, pretending to think. "Well, okay, yeah, maybe I would call it blackmail."

Grumbling under her breath, Melissa controlled her anger, picked up the bottles, and staggered down the path. *I have no one to blame but myself*, she admitted. *So I admire Jackson? And who wouldn't? Look at the way he ate that oyster. He's risking his life to get us a new source of food.*

As she walked, Mel realized that Jackson wasn't the problem. He was only the symptom. *I'm the problem. I'm such a wimp!*

Eric

I hate taking advantage of her, but it's every man for himself. And she's such an easy target. It's almost not fair. Almost? Wait. Who am I kidding, I don't hate it at all.

But look, there's another level to this. You have to look at our situation from a higher perspective. This whole survive-in-the-jungle thing is kind of like a huge scientific experiment. You put a bunch of kids on an island. And then you see what kinds of character traits prove to be most useful. This could end up being a really important breakthrough in, uh, psyche, uh psyche, uh . . . *psychiatry*? Or is it *psychology*? What's the difference? I've never been real clear on that. Maybe I should have Lex look into it for me.

He'd love that. It'd make him feel important. See what a nice guy I can be?

Anyway, here's what I'm getting at. Everybody loves Melissa. But where's that get her? She's carrying water while I'm sitting here eating tasty tropical fruits. When the chips are down, I'm gonna be all rested and ready to do what's necessary for the team. And Melissa's gonna be all worn-out and useless.

So when you get right down to it, who's really the selfless guy?

Exactly. *Me.*

See the point I'm making? Me, I'm all about the science. So even if I look all lazy and manipulative? It's just a front. Could I be like Melissa, the one everybody likes? Of course I could. Any moron can be likeable. Nah, see, it's like I'm sacrificing my precious reputation for integrity and honesty and, you know, all the rest of that stuff . . . just to further the boundaries of human knowledge.

Hey, somebody's gotta do it.

Jackson was okay just sitting in the shade, watching cloud elephants morph into sumo wrestlers. Under Lex's orders, that was all he was supposed to do. There was a theory that physical exertion might cause the toxins to spread faster. If there *were* any toxins. It felt strange to just sit around and be stared at, but there really wasn't any other way to monitor the effects of the shellfish.

So this is what life is like as a scientific specimen. Lex peered frequently into his eyes, his nose, his mouth, and at his own watch. It would be comical if the circumstances weren't so serious. They desperately needed more sources for food. And some staple items besides fruit. Eating fruit for breakfast, lunch, and dinner had the potential to turn their new latrine into a river.

"How do you feel?" Lex finally asked.

Jackson squirmed in his seat and said, "Same as when you asked me five minutes ago."

"It's been three hours," Lex said, pointing to his watch. "If there's a problem, you'll probably start puking your guts out anytime now."

Great, Jackson thought. *Good to know.*

Eric quickly located Nathan, who was still walking

gingerly. He found his intended victim waddling behind the wrecked plane, searching for a place to crash. When the miserable guy finally eased his sore behind onto the sand, the look of relief on his face was hilarious. But Eric wasn't going to let him relax for long.

He jumped from behind the plane and shouted, "Nathan!"

Nathan lurched in surprise and grimaced in pain. "Ahhhhh! Ouchhh! Don't do that."

"I've been looking all over for you," Eric said innocently. "Daley needs some help." He pulled Nathan to his feet.

Nathan winced in agony. "Leave me alone," he begged. "I'm dying here."

Eric whispered, "Don't show pain . . . unless you want everybody to know about your fungus."

"It's not a fungus!" Nathan insisted.

"C'mon," Eric said. Like a Boy Scout helping a little old lady across the street, he guided Nathan back toward the beach, where Daley was waiting. The poor boy just kept whimpering, and Eric tried not to smile.

Is this going to be our fate? Dying slowly of gruesome, painful skin diseases? Every step was like a centipede picnic in his pants, and the fiery sensation shot up his belly. Nathan knew that Daley had an awful rash, too, and maybe it wasn't allergies. Daley's efforts to get them clean clothes helped some, but he could see the bug bites and leech marks on everyone. They probably all had hidden crud they weren't talking about.

Speaking of talking, how could I be so stupid as to tell Eric? Now he's got something on me!

It was a surefire guarantee that he'd try to use it to pry something out of Nathan. But right now Nathan had worse things to think about.

A searing shot of pain made Nathan whimper. Then he spotted Daley walking toward him. He plastered a smile over his grimace. The redhead stood proudly over a pile of slimy seaweed, kicking it with her toe. It looked like something out of the movie *Alien*. Nathan tried to walk normally, and he gutted out the pain until he was able to stand still again. Then he had to watch the flies buzz around this monumental pile of slimy greenery.

"Check this out," Eric said. "Daley has a brilliant idea. Tell him."

She gestured excitedly as she explained, "I can't believe we didn't think of this before. We can *eat* seaweed."

"Fabulous," Nathan said. "Can I go now?"

"I'm serious. You can eat seaweed."

"You can?" Nathan asked doubtfully.

"Yes! I learned about it in oceanography class. It's like floating salad."

"Then why's it called sea*weed*?" Nathan asked.

"You've eaten it," Daley said. "It's also called carrageen. They use it to thicken lots of foods. Some fast-food milk shakes have it. There's major vitamins here—we just have to rinse off the salt."

"It's a great idea," Eric agreed. "Nathan's gonna help you collect all this green gold and bring it to the fire pit."

Daley frowned and asked, "What about you?"

He waved his hand as he backed away. "Oh, I'm on water duty. Gotta keep the H_2O flowing, right?" With that, Eric jogged off.

"What a total load," Nathan complained.

"Whatever," Daley said, who was too enthused over her

discovery to be unhappy. "Bring this up and start rinsing. I'll collect more."

Nathan stared at the mammoth pile of bulbous green things. This was going to involve a lot of bending. And bending made the seams of his pants move around. And every time the seams moved, it felt like a saw blade biting into his flesh.

But what was he gonna do?

Daley peered closely at him and said, "Unless you've joined the Eric McGorrill International League of Laziness and can't do it either."

"No, no, I'm good." Nathan gritted his teeth and bent low for an armful of slimy seaweed.

"I'm alive," Jackson announced, holding up a just-opened oyster. "Let's eat."

"Eeeyyeew!" Taylor shouted, making a face of disgust.

Nathan got the impression that Taylor was just using the whole oyster thing to get attention. Useless skills like knowing the best place to get your legs waxed just didn't help you much around here. Truth was, with all the fancy restaurants her rich parents took her to, she probably ate oysters all the time.

But with Taylor, you never knew.

Jackson banged on one of the coolers for emphasis, and everyone applauded him. They were enthusiastic . . . until they saw the shellfish. Daley and Lex had tried to make the slimy mollusks look as appetizing as possible, but oysters were what they were.

"Wow," Nathan looked closely at an oyster, "it really does look like snot."

"But it's not," Lex insisted.

Taylor said, "That's what he said. It's *snot*." Then she laughed loudly and looked around to see if anybody else got the joke.

"Get it?" Eric said, sucking up to her as usual. "It's not? It's . . . *snot?*"

Daley gave Eric and Taylor a big fake smile. "Hey, that was a pretty funny joke. Back in fourth grade." She put her hands on her hips. "Everybody, just stop it! You're acting like babies. I've eaten tons of oysters. Think of 'em as little fish."

"Yeah. Little fish that we're eating alive," Eric added. He switched into a high voice. "Help! Help! They're sucking my brains out with their horrible giant tongues!" Nobody laughed, so he shut up.

Taylor held up a finger. "Excuse me, I still don't get the part about eating them alive. Why can't they just start out dead . . . like meat you buy at a store?"

"You know, Taylor," Nathan said, "I hate to break it to you, but the beef you get at the store used to be part of a living creature, too. It's called a cow."

Taylor stared blankly at him.

Melissa jumped in to explain, "Seriously, though, you have to eat oysters when they're still alive. If they sit around, they go bad real fast."

"Great. Like I wasn't grossed-out enough already?" Taylor made a big show of wrinkling her nose and rolling her eyes.

There was a loud rumble—somebody's stomach grumbling. Everybody looked at Eric.

"Now that I think about it? Suddenly snot doesn't seem so bad," Eric said. It was hard to tell if he was making a joke or not.

Nathan kept looking at the disgusting little puddle of goo in the shell. He wasn't sure if he was *quite* that hungry yet. "Should we cook 'em?" he said.

Lex shook his head. "Cooking might burn off nutrients, and we need everything we can get."

"How do you know these things?" Eric asked.

"I think he just makes stuff up," Taylor said.

Frustrated, Daley waved her arms. "I'm telling you, oysters aren't bad, and Jackson survived, so—"

"Whatever!" Eric snapped. "Look, the heck with it, I'm starving to death here." He grabbed one of the oysters and slurped it down. Everyone leaned forward to watch him chomp and swallow.

He chewed for a minute. Eventually his eyebrows went up as though in surprise.

"Mmmm! Little chewy, but pretty decent!" he said. "Could use some oyster sauce, though."

Melissa shook her head sadly. "I don't think I'm desperate enough."

Eric scoffed at them and grabbed another oyster. "C'mon! Fear is not a factor here! If I can do it, anybody can." He slurped down the live creature in his hand.

Jackson frowned at Taylor, wondering what he could do to get her to eat. Seaweed was also on the menu tonight, so he picked up a slice of that. He rolled some oyster meat into it and offered it to the blond girl. "This is better than anything at one of your fancy L.A. restaurants."

She looked doubtfully at him, and the others stopped cracking oysters long enough to listen. "Don't think of it as raw oyster," Jackson said. "Think of it as . . . sushi."

Taylor blinked at him. Suddenly she smiled brightly, her even white teeth sparkling in the sun. "Sushi? I love sushi."

"So isn't sushi just raw fish wrapped in seaweed?" Jackson asked.

Her eyes moved from the seaweed to the oysters then to the seaweed then to the oysters. "Yeah," she said finally. "I guess."

"Then pretend it's Friday night, and you're living large."

"Only thing missing is the rice," Nathan said.

"Oh, I don't do carbs," she reminded him.

Nathan had almost forgotten. They had dated briefly, but every time they went out, she had been on some kind of new dietary restriction. For a while she'd been a vegetarian, and then for a while there was no dairy, and then . . . well, it had been hard to keep track.

Jackson smiled and offered Taylor the oyster roll. "Then you're good to go."

She cautiously took the sushi roll and bit into it. Everyone watched as she slowly reacted to the two new food sources. Taylor chewed thoughtfully, nodded her head, and proclaimed, "Sushi!"

The whole gang laughed, and Jackson quickly made another roll for her. Now the others were getting into the seaweed as a side dish to the oysters, and it almost seemed like a festive night out in a fancy restaurant.

Finally Nathan grabbed one of the oysters, shut his eyes, and dumped the thing in his mouth. The slithering action wasn't so cool. But the taste . . . hey, not bad!

It can't get much better than this, Eric thought as he stretched out on his beach towel. *No work, but I've accomplished a lot—learning two secrets about my fellow survivors. Those secrets put food in my stomach and worked*

miracles in the camp, even if I did nothing. This is effective management.

Melissa was still hauling water after dinner, and she hurried up to him. "Enough, okay?" she whispered. "I've been doing your job *and* my job all day. Would you please help me now?"

"Ummm . . . no, sorry," he answered, looking pained. "Maybe I can get Jackson to help. I'm pretty sure you'd like that, wouldn't you?"

Melissa scowled at him and said, "I hate you." She stormed off, heading toward the fire pit, and Eric chuckled at her helplessness.

A moment later, Taylor ran up to him, all excited. "Eric, come with me!" she insisted. "I want to get more of those yummy oysters."

He nodded as if he was listening, but he was really looking for someone on whom he could unload this task. He spotted Nathan lounging in the shade of the plane, and figured this was a good job for an ex-boyfriend.

With a smile, Eric steered Taylor toward his helpless victim. "Sounds like a party," he said, "but more of a Nathan kind of thing."

Easily diverted, Taylor grabbed Nathan's hand and started hauling him toward the tide pools. "C'mon. You can carry way more than me," she told him.

Nathan winced in pain and shuffled gingerly into the craggy tide pools. He glanced over his shoulder at Eric and muttered, "I hate you."

Eric tried not to laugh out loud, although it was pretty funny. *Who says Jackson is the leader!* he mused. *I'm the one who knows how to delegate.*

He took a step, but his stomach took about a twenty-foot leap. Eric staggered and doubled over, unsure where the sudden nausea had come from. His throat was dry and wet at the same time, and he was sweating like someone doing real work. Eric took a step toward the ocean, hoping it would clear his head, but his whole body felt disconnected and numb.

Just gotta rest, he thought as he slumped onto the sand.

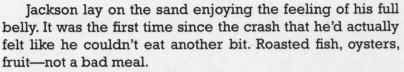

Jackson lay on the sand enjoying the feeling of his full belly. It was the first time since the crash that he'd actually felt like he couldn't eat another bit. Roasted fish, oysters, fruit—not a bad meal.

He was a little worried, though. He'd lost two fishhooks in the last day. Each time, he had announced to the group that he was running low on fishhooks. And each time a new hook made from an earring had showed up in his tent. Along with a brief note from the "friend." Same yellow paper, same red pen.

How many earrings could be left? They'd be in trouble if he ran out of hooks. He wanted to talk to the "friend"— maybe brainstorm about coming up with another source of hooks. But who was the mysterious person? And where were the earrings coming from?

The second fishhook had appeared during a period when he'd been with Lex the entire time. So he could rule the younger boy out.

Which left . . . who? Eric? Eric seemed the likely candidate. Eric was all about knowing more than he let on. Probably stealing earrings from the girls' tent, though. That wasn't a long-term solution.

Speaking of Eric . . .

What was he doing over there? He was lying in the sand groaning. Jackson shook his head. Probably coming up with another excuse to avoid work.

FIFTEEN

The moment she turned on the video camera, Melissa knew she had to make a decision. She could see Jackson at the fire pit, cleaning up after their meal. He was alone, maybe for the first time that day.

Melissa

I can't let Eric blackmail me anymore, but I don't want him telling Jackson that I like him. If anybody is going to tell him, it has to be me. Yikes.

A moment later, she walked up to Jackson, who was piling empty oyster shells on a rock. "Hey," he said.

"I'll help," she answered. They continued to pick shells

off the beach while Melissa tried to assemble the right words in her head. After a beat, she decided to just go for it before she lost her nerve.

"Jackson," she began, "I want to—"

Eric staggered by, doing his best I'm-too-tired-to-walk imitation. "Eric!" Jackson called. "Give us a hand."

Eric rubbed his stomach. "Uh, I'm not feeling so hot."

"Yeah, right," Jackson answered. "Grab some of the—"

Melissa didn't want Eric hanging around during her big moment, especially since he wouldn't be useful anyway. So she jumped up and steered him in another direction. "It's okay," she insisted. "If Eric feels bad, he should relax."

He should win an award for this performance.

"Find some shade and lie down," she said, doing her best to sound more sincere than she felt. Then, lowering her voice to a whisper, she added, "And go away!"

Eric groaned. "Seriously, I don't feel good."

"Oh, please." Melissa gave him a push to send him staggering down the beach.

She took a breath, ready to start her big confession all over again—when Lex ran over to the fire pit. "I'll help!" he told Jackson.

Frustrated, Melissa kicked the sand. *There goes my moment.*

Nathan got some relief from his burning rash in the salty coolness of the tide pool. But he got no relief from Taylor, who couldn't stop extolling the virtues of her new favorite food.

"There's, like, no end to them!" she exclaimed, holding an oyster in each hand. "We can make California oyster rolls with fruit, and oyster salad, and oyster kabobs, and even oyster soup. Yum, oyster soup! Wouldn't that be awesome?"

"Yeah, awesome," Nathan murmured, settling deeper into the calm pool. Still babbling, Taylor went on gathering oysters. "Take your time," he told her, "I'm lovin' the water."

Even chili dogs with pineapples never laid me this low, Eric thought as he slumped onto the sand near the wrecked airplane. He dabbed the sweat off his forehead, even though he was shivering, and wondered whether he was going to heave. Barfing might be a relief . . . for the churning in his gut and his aching head.

He didn't see Daley walk up until she hovered over him. "Hey, give me a hand," she demanded. "We need more seaweed. Who knew Taylor was gonna love the stuff?"

"I . . . uh, I'm feeling really lousy," he told her.

Daley rolled her eyes with annoyance. "Aw, c'mon, Eric, you gotta start coming up with better excuses."

"It's no excuse—"

She waved at him in disgust. "Yeah, right. Forget it." With a scowl, Daley marched off, and Eric crawled into the cabin of the wrecked plane.

Maybe I should tell somebody else, he thought miserably, *after I lie down for a minute. Besides, I already told somebody else. She didn't listen. They don't believe me . . . anymore . . .*

Taylor had collected enough oysters to feed them all for a week, but Nathan still didn't want to move from the cool, salty water. *I'm probably not doing my rash any good, but too bad.* Lex had already harvested the oysters here, and nobody bothered him.

"That should do it . . . for now," Taylor said proudly. "Let's get these back to camp." When Nathan didn't move, she stamped her foot impatiently. "What are you doing?"

Leave now? No can do. Nathan was whupped. He couldn't bring himself to move, not even to help Taylor get enthused about her new survival diet. It was awfully embarrassing, but he was way past embarrassment. The temporary relief felt too good to give up.

"Uh, I've, uh, hmm . . . I've got a situation," he stammered. Taylor just looked at him. "Okay, I was stupid and wore wet shorts all day. Now I've got a nasty rash that makes poison ivy seem like baby powder. There, I said it. Now laugh and go away so the saltwater can do its job."

Taylor put her hands on her hips and looked thoughtfully at him. "That's your big situation? A rash? Is it contagious?"

"No!" Nathan shouted.

"Then I can help," Taylor said with a smile.

A full stomach took away some of the pangs, but Melissa was still bummed over losing her opportunity to talk to Jackson. Plus, Eric was still blackmailing her and shirking work, and she didn't have control of anything in her life. *Forget the food and water, I have to get a lot tougher to survive emotionally. I can't let people run over me and use me, especially here . . . where it's life and death.*

I'm thankful we have food and water . . . and a good leader. But I still have to look out for myself.

"Mel?"

"Huh?"

"What do you think of this one?" Lex asked, holding up an oyster shell.

She and Lex were sorting through the oyster pile, wondering if they could use the shells for anything. The only things that suggested themselves were ashtrays, or candy dishes. And since none of them smoked and there wasn't any candy . . .

A shadow passed over her, and she looked up.

Melissa wasn't expecting comic relief from anyone, especially from Nathan, but she burst out laughing when she saw him wearing Taylor's shortest skirt. He dumped an armload of fresh oysters by the fire and smiled sheepishly.

"Something you want to tell us?" Lex asked with amusement.

He answered calmly, "No, but since you asked, Taylor loaned me this because I've got a rash on my legs."

"Prickly heat," Taylor said loftily. "Call it 'prickly heat.' Rash sounds like you've got a flesh-eating disease. And before you give that back, wash it. Twice."

Melissa chuckled and said, "Very sensible, Nathan . . . and cute."

"I won't be climbing any coconut trees in this outfit," he added.

"Where is everybody?" Taylor demanded. "I want to start cracking these babies open."

"Jackson went with Daley to get more seaweed," Melissa said. "I don't know where Eric is."

Nathan grumbled, "Probably sleeping. That guy is a piece of work."

Jackson walked up, carrying a fresh load of seaweed. "If you're talking about Eric, I just saw him . . . in the plane."

"His favorite napping place," Nathan grumbled.

Within a few minutes, everybody was at the pit, except

for Eric. After they'd finished ragging on Nathan for his new attire, Taylor began to hand out oysters.

"C'mon, get cracking!" she ordered. "Just think, if we hadn't crashed, I never would have discovered how much I like oysters."

"Wow," Daley said. "That makes it all worthwhile."

"I feel bad eating without Eric," Lex said. He glanced over his shoulder at the wrecked plane farther down the beach.

"Don't, it's his own fault," Melissa said.

"But it's weird," Lex said. "He never misses a meal."

Those gathered around the fire pit looked at one another, and Nathan knew that somebody had to take a stroll. Lex was right about Eric not missing a meal. No matter what bogus ailment he complained about, he always made a remarkable recovery at dinnertime. Now that Nathan had gotten relief from the rubbing and chafing, he was good to go.

"I'll find him," Nathan volunteered. "I don't mind. I can walk again!"

He did a little skip as he strolled off, careful not to let his cover-up fly too high. Behind him, he heard Taylor mutter, "I can never wear that skirt again."

In the waning light of day, Nathan approached the wreck of 29 DWN, thinking it was awfully quiet around the ghostly airplane. Maybe it just sounded that way because of all the laughter and conversation at the other end of the beach. Eric must really be tired to miss a loud party like that.

Nathan stopped outside the door and scowled at Eric, who was curled in a ball on the floor of the plane. "Hey, dude! The act is getting old."

The clod didn't budge, so Nathan went on, "By the way, you wanna tell about my rash? Too late. Everybody knows. Look, I'm wearing a skirt. I have no shame!"

When Eric didn't move again, Nathan nudged him with his foot. "C'mon, Eric, get up."

Eric's breathing sounded labored. "Eric? Hey!"

Nathan tried to shake Eric awake, but it was no go. He listened more closely at Eric's chest and heard definite wheezing, plus the teen was as clammy as a snake.

"Guys!" Nathan yelled. Nathan felt a stab of panic. He was no great fan of Eric. But this was serious. He dashed out of the fuselage, waving his arms and shouting, "Guys! Get down here . . . now!"

SIXTEEN

Now this is vacation!

Now this is vacation!
Eric was floating on a rubber raft in the open
sea. Back and forth, up and down, swaying with
every wave. Each of his limbs moved independently, and he
wondered vaguely if he was tied to four different rafts. Oh
well, it didn't matter, because his body was liquid—like the
waves. He couldn't move on his own at all. He could only go
with the gentle current ... and let it sweep him along.

Shadows passed over Eric, and it began to rain. A wave
dashed him against a rock—or maybe it was the bottom of
the ocean. Everything began to spin. *Whirlpool!* Around
and around the dark clouds flew, and people were yelling
at him. Their voices were spinning, too, and they asked silly
questions.

"How do you feel?"

"Everything's spinning," he croaked.

It was all so confusing, and the stormy waves were making

him seasick. Eric liked it better before . . . in the sunshine . . . on the gentle waves.

Melissa paced nervously as Jackson and Nathan put Eric inside the boys' tent. She didn't know how that was going to help Eric, but it made them feel better to move him from the plane.

He told us he was sick, and we all ignored him. Yeah, he's a lousy friend sometimes. But so are we all. Oh, please, don't let anything happen to him.

Daley had taken charge, which was good. For once, Jackson seemed at a loss.

Sticking her head out of the tent, Daley reported, "I don't think he's got a fever, but he's dehydrated. We need water."

Nathan and Jackson looked at each other, but it was Lex who said, "I'll get it." The boy ran off.

Melissa tried not to wring her hands when she asked, "What's wrong with him?"

"I don't know," Nathan admitted. "He's got cramps, and he's itchy. He's having trouble breathing, too."

They stood around helplessly until Lex returned with a water bottle. "It's gotta be the oysters," the kid said, "but we all ate them!"

Taylor gasped with alarm. "Are we all going to die?"

Melissa frowned and shook her head, because something about this was oddly familiar. *I've been here before,* she thought. Like a whirlwind, Melissa grabbed the water bottle and dove into the tent. Nathan followed her inside, where it was already pretty crowded with Daley and Jackson.

Eric lay on a blanket, moaning and speaking gibberish. Melissa leaned over him and demanded, "Tell me how you feel."

"Throat's tight," he murmured.

"Look at his skin," Melissa said.

"What?" Daley asked.

"His skin!" Melissa ripped Eric's shirt off his scrawny body, and they all gasped when they saw that his stomach and chest were covered with ugly red blotches. Some of them were raised, like on a topographic globe.

"Hives," Nathan said.

Melissa shook her head. "He's not sick; he's allergic."

Daley leaned over Eric and yelled, "Eric, are you allergic to shellfish?"

"I . . . I don't know. Never had any," he muttered.

"That's gotta be it," Nathan declared.

Melissa whispered to the others, "My cousin almost died from an allergic reaction."

"What do we do?" Daley asked, but no one had an answer.

"The first-aid kit," Melissa said. "Maybe there's—"

Nathan didn't wait for her to finish her sentence. He charged out of the tent and ran to get the old duffel bag.

Time stood still in that dreary tent as they listened to Eric's labored breathing. Melissa talked calmly to her classmate and tried to tell him that everything would be okay. His eyes were still open, but he mumbled. She knew he wasn't listening anymore. Daley and Jackson didn't look very convinced that everything would be okay, and that didn't do much for her coping skills.

My last words to him were angry, and I ignored him when he needed help. After all we've gone through, we can't lose you, Eric. Stay awake!

Nathan must have run like the wind in Taylor's skirt, because he returned only a few moments later with the first-aid kit. He zipped open the bag and rummaged through the contents. "What do we need?"

Daley grabbed the booklet and began to read. "Allergies ... allergies?"

Jackson turned to Melissa and asked, "What happened to your cousin?"

"It was from a bee sting," she answered, trying to remember every detail. "But it was all the same symptoms. Rash, cramps, trouble breathing."

"What did you do for it?" Nathan asked.

Melissa swallowed. "Uh. We took him to the hospital."

"But ... he'd have been okay if you hadn't ... right?"

Melissa didn't say anything.

"He's gonna get better after a while, right?" Daley said. "I mean ... it's just allergies."

Melissa kept looking at Eric, not speaking.

"What?" Daley said finally.

"They said if we'd brought my cousin in fifteen minutes later, he'd have been dead."

Jackson was pacing up and down the beach near the boys' tent. Lex poked his head out of the zippered flap of the tent. "He's really looking bad," he said.

"You got any ideas?" Jackson said. "You always seem to know everything."

"I'm not a doctor, Jackson," the younger boy said.

Jackson flushed. The kid was right. Maybe he was expecting too much from him.

Taylor came out holding her hands helplessly in the air. "What are we gonna do?" she said.

Daley looked out the door, too. "You're the leader, Jackson. Think of something!"

Jackson shook his head. Everybody was looking at him now. Jackson's stomach felt sick. This was really bad. He felt like he was carrying a huge weight on his shoulders, a weight that was about to crush him.

"I can't take this anymore," Taylor said. "This is just too—" She waved her hands in the air, seemingly at a loss for words.

"Let me see the first-aid kit," Jackson said. Daley brought it out of the tent and Jackson scrabbled through it. Sutures, bandages, scissors, antibiotic ointment—they'd be in great shape if anybody scraped a knee. But an allergic reaction to shellfish? There might be something in here that would help . . . but how would he even know?

He shook his head, dropped the kit in the sand. Everybody stared helplessly at the small plastic box.

"I can't deal," Taylor said finally. "I just can't deal." She disappeared into the shadows.

"Boy, she's a big help," Daley said.

"Hey, it's not like the rest of us are doing much better," Nathan said.

He had a point. Jackson was feeling completely useless. How could he pretend to be a leader when he couldn't help anybody with anything? It was a joke really . . . the whole idea of him being a leader.

Tired of the helpless feeling, he went back into the tent, stared down at Eric's prone body. Melissa had been sitting there on the ground next to Eric the whole time. She probably had more reason to dislike Eric than anybody on the island. And yet here she was, sticking with him like he was her best friend. Jackson sort of felt like saying something to her— "you're a good friend," or something like that. But it just didn't seem like the right moment.

It didn't seem like the right moment because Eric started wiggling and jerking.

"What's that?" Jackson said.

"I think he's having a seizure," Lex said, sticking his head back in the flap.

Jackson started rubbing his temples. What was he going to do?

Daley and Nathan walked back into the tent, looking at him expectantly. Suddenly the tent just seemed *way* too crowded, and Jackson felt like he couldn't quite catch his breath.

Lex's head disappeared from the flap. He was gone for a minute, then he came back, held something out to Jackson.

"I brought this back in," Lex said, handing the first-aid kit to Jackson. "Didn't seem like it would do much good lying out there in the sand."

Jackson took it distractedly.

"Maybe you should look through it again," Lex said.

"I already looked," Jackson snapped.

But he glanced down at it anyway.

Which is when he noticed the corner of a piece of yellow paper sticking out of the kit.

He opened the kit quickly. Inside was a familiar-looking note. The yellow paper, the red pen, the block letters.

"He's gone into anaphylactic shock," the note read. "He needs a shot of adrenaline."

Beneath the note was the familiar signature:

"A friend."

Jackson read the note silently, then wadded up the note and dropped it on the floor. "Anaphylactic shock," he muttered.

"What?" Daley said.

"He needs adrenaline."

Nathan grabbed the kit. "That's right! Anaphylactic shock! I saw that on *ER* once." He looked through the kit for a minute, came out with a small plastic tube. "Yes!"

Daley grabbed it from him. "What is it?"

"It's an injector," Nathan said. "See, there's a big needle. You just jab it into him. Then this spring shoots the dose into him."

"Gross!" a voice said. Taylor was standing in the doorway of the tent.

Everyone ignored her.

"Here, you do it," Daley said, handing the injector back to Nathan.

"Hey, I'm not a big needle guy," Nathan said. "Why don't *you* do it?"

"No, *you* do it."

"No, *you* do it."

"No, *you* do it!"

"You're kinda freakin' me out," Taylor said.

"Guys!" Jackson held up his hands.

Everybody went silent, waiting for him to speak.

Taylor pointed at Eric. "I think he just passed out."

She was right. He lay limply now, not moving at all. Jackson couldn't even tell if he was breathing.

Nathan held out the injector toward Jackson. "Here."

Jackson looked at it nervously. Sticking pieces of sharp metal into human flesh creeped him out a little. And besides, what if it was the wrong thing? What if it killed Eric? Jackson felt this jittery, weak sensation in his arms. He really just wasn't sure he could do it.

"Uh . . ." Jackson said.

"Oh, for godsake!" Melissa grabbed the injector, ripped off the plastic sheath covering the needle, and plunged it deep into Eric's thigh.

Everyone held their breath as they watched the medicine ebb slowly out of the tube and into Eric's thigh.

After removing the needle, Melissa massaged Eric's leg, but he just lay there as if he was way past feeling any pain.

"Now what?" Daley asked nervously.

"Now we wait," Melissa said, wiping the sweat off her brow.

Did I inject him in time? Melissa thought. *Or did we waste too much time ... ignoring him? This isn't a joke anymore ... it never was. We gotta stop the head games and get serious.*

Taylor spoke for most of them when she whined, "I want to go home."

Daley nodded with sympathy. Until now, their adventure had been full of danger and foolish risks, but she had never felt so completely helpless. Watching Eric suffer made her feel small. . . . How could they ever be in control of their lives in this primitive place? Even Jackson, Mr. Cool, looked a little bit shaken. His face was pale and his long fingers were trembling slightly.

With a sigh, Daley went back into the boys' tent. Eric's condition hadn't changed. Melissa, Jackson, and Lex were watching his every movement, and now it was the four of them watching. It hadn't been more than twenty minutes since the injection, but it felt like hours.

Suddenly, Eric's hand lifted and touched the wet cloth they had put on his forehead. He blinked and looked around, and his eyes settled on Melissa. "Was that a dream," he rasped, "or did you stab me in the freakin' leg?"

Everybody let out an enormous sigh, and Lex and Jackson slumped to the ground. Melissa took another packet from the first-aid kit and handed it to Daley. "After we took my cousin to the hospital, they said to give him antihistamines for twelve hours," she said wearily. "I guess the adrenaline doesn't last long. Give him these."

"Okay," Daley answered. She watched as her friend stood up and walked outside. *Talk about taking leadership and bold action*, Daley thought. *Mel really came through.*

Eric stared at them, looking confused until Jackson said, "Dude, she just saved your life."

"Well," Daley said, giving Jackson a significant look, "she had a little help."

Jackson had an odd look on his face.

"You okay?" Daley said.

Jackson looked around at everybody, his eyes pausing for a moment on each face. "Was anybody alone with the first-aid kit?" he said.

She frowned. "What do you mean?"

"Was anybody alone with the first-aid kit?"

It was kind of an odd question. "I don't think so. Why?"

He didn't answer. Instead, he scowled, then walked out of the tent like something was bugging him.

The more she saw of the guy, the weirder he seemed.

Melissa ended the day down by the fire pit, boiling, straining, and pouring water as usual. After the gamble she had taken with Eric's life, it felt good to be doing something simple and brainless.

She was a little surprised when Eric shuffled toward her, a sleeping bag draped around his shoulders.

Nathan hurried past them with Taylor in hot pursuit. "You are *so* not keeping that!" she yelled at him.

"C'mon, just a little longer," Nathan begged. He tugged protectively at his skirt and kept on jogging.

Melissa looked at Eric and asked, "What are you doing up?"

Eric managed a wan smile and pulled two half-filled water jugs from under the sleeping bag. He set them by the fire—it was the first water he had collected in a long time. Not that they were exactly full or anything. But still. At least he had made the effort.

"Thanks," said Eric softly. "I guess I kind of owe you, huh?" When he tried to pick up more bottles to return to the well, Melissa stopped him.

"You're welcome," she told Eric. She took his trembling arm and led him to a seat on the log. Finally, Eric had a good excuse not to work.

She took a step toward the plane. "Anything I can get for you?"

"Nah." He pointed at the camera sitting over on the other side of the fire ring. "Hey, make sure you lay it all down in your video diary. You'll want to make sure you get credit for saving my life."

For a minute Melissa felt embarrassed. But then she looked up and said, "Do you think that's what life is about? Getting credit?"

Eric looked at her curiously, like she had asked him an extremely strange question. "Um. I'll go get some more water," he said.

This time she didn't stop him.

Melissa

As soon as he feels better, he's gonna go right back to being a jerk, but it's nice to know there's a human buried somewhere deep in there. Very deep. It's also nice to know that Jackson isn't the only strong one around here.

Everybody else was afraid to stick a needle into another human being. But I did it. It was like my instincts took over, and wham. Even Jackson looked all freaked out when Nathan tried to hand him the needle.

Jackson . . . it seems like I keep coming back to that subject. Well, I'm gonna have to face that one soon. But in the meantime, it just feels nice to have done something good. Would I have ever done something like that before we crashed on this island? I don't think so.

Melissa was just turning off the camera when she heard someone clear his throat behind her.

Melissa whirled around, the smile dying on her face. It was Jackson.

"Oh, Jackson!" she said. She flushed. "You scared me. Were you listening to . . ." Her voice trailed off. She pointed at the camera.

He shook his head distractedly. For a moment there was an awkward silence.

"So look," he said, "there's something I need to talk to you about."

She blinked, then felt a nervous smile break out on her face. Was it possible he was feeling the same thing she was? Oh, man, that would rock! "Yeah?" she said. "I'm so glad to hear that. Because I wanted to talk to you, too."

Jackson looked around like he was checking to see if

anybody might be in earshot of their conversation. Was it possible? Melissa felt her pulse quicken. "Uh . . . you first," she said.

"No, go ahead," he said.

"You first."

He looked around again, moved a step closer. Melissa felt her heartbeat quicken. "So . . ." he said. "You were with Eric the whole time, right?"

She frowned. "Yeah . . ."

"Were you alone with the first-aid kit?"

"Huh?" She felt the excitement drain out of her. What was he getting at?

"The first-aid kit. Were you alone with it?"

She shrugged. "I don't know."

"It was in the tent, then we took it outside, then I dropped it on the sand. Somewhere in there somebody had to have been alone with it."

Melissa felt her breath drain slowly out of her lungs. She shrugged. Suddenly she felt really tired. "I don't . . . I don't know, Jackson."

Jackson shook his head. "This is so weird."

"What?" she said. "What's weird?"

He stared at the ground for a while. Almost like he'd forgotten she was there. "Nothing," he said finally.

Then he turned and started to walk away. After he'd gone about ten paces, he stopped, turned, looked at her. His eyes seemed to glow in the gloomy dusk.

"Sorry," he said. "You had something you wanted to talk to me about?"

"It's been a long day," Melissa said dejectedly. "It'll keep."

Jackson looked at her for a moment, then abruptly turned and walked off.

I am such a wimp, she thought. *I am such a wimp.*

SEVENTEEN

The next day, it was like the storm had passed, and the skies were suddenly clear again. Lex looked down the beach, where he spotted a few of the older kids. They weren't moping or complaining as usual—they were goofing off. It made Lex wonder why he was working so hard. He decided that he couldn't get mad at them.

After Eric got well, everyone got well. Lex figured they had dodged this bullet—but they might not dodge the next one. What would happen next time somebody got sick? Or broke an arm? Or whatever? There was a sense that they were out of danger. But the truth was, they wouldn't really be out of danger until they were rescued.

So that's what Lex was concentrating on. Let the big kids goof off. He was going to get them off this island! He was going to get them rescued.

He stepped back to admire his work. Up close, it just looked like a bunch of junk—flooring from the plane, strips of fabric and metal, some coconut husks—anything he could find.

Eric wandered by, sucking on a bottle of water. "Nice junk pile, dude," he said.

"Step back," Lex said.

"Huh?"

"Step back," Lex said again, motioning to Eric to join him about ten paces from the huge collection of material.

Eric shrugged and joined Lex.

"Now look," Lex said. From here, Eric would be able to make out what he was doing.

"Whoa! Sweet!" It was a large sign. Eric read it out loud. "SOS. WE'RE ALIVE. 29 DWN."

"I'm going to set it up so that planes will be able to see it when they fly over."

"Cool." Eric took another sip from the bottle. "Where you gonna put it?"

"I'm not sure. Maybe stretch it between a couple of trees? Then I'll light it with torches."

"Torches? I didn't know we had torches."

"We don't . . ." Lex said. ". . . yet."

Eric looked up in the air, as though searching the sky for planes. In the entire week they'd been here, not one single plane had flown over. He raised his eyebrows slightly.

"So, look, I was wondering if maybe you could help me—"

"Whew!" Eric said. "Yeah, right now's a little tough. Kinda busy. So, yeah, no, probably not right now. Maybe, uh . . . later?"

Eric shuffled off toward the water, unbuttoned his shirt, and jumped into the surf.

Great, Lex thought. *Glad he's got his priorities straight.*

But it wasn't like anybody else seemed to be any

different. Even his workaholic big sister was lounging on the dunes with Nathan, playing tic-tac-toe. Daley hadn't even said good morning to him yet.

Maybe she hadn't forgotten what day it was. Maybe she would still remember. He couldn't blame her for forgetting what day it was. People lost track of time in situations like this.

Taylor was intently building a sand mansion, Melissa was picking flowers, and Eric floated on life preservers in the sea. *Sure, we have all the necessities,* Lex thought. *Clean water and good sources of food. Especially if we find more ways to eat seaweed. But we can't lose our edge—we can't stop pushing ourselves.*

The only person who wasn't lounging around was Jackson, who was nowhere to be seen.

Definitely in vacation mode today. *Oh, well. Let them play. They're older. They get more stressed than I do.* With a sigh, Lex put down his hammer and nails and picked up the video camera.

Lex

We've been stuck here a week. Nobody says it, but I know we're all worried that we haven't seen any sign of a search. No boats, no planes, nothing. It's scary. So far we've done an okay job of surviving, but we've got a new problem. We're all going a little nuts from being so bored.

It's starting to turn into kind of a routine now. Fruit, fruit, fruit. Fish, fish, fish. Oysters, oysters, oysters. Swim. Get water. Gather firewood. Swim some more. Then more fruit, more fish, more oysters.

Eric's sickness gave us a little break from
the monotony. But once things settle down,
everybody's liable to start wigging out.

⚙

Daley yawned and rolled over in the sand. She and
Nathan were lounging on the dunes, watching the camp
and playing tic-tac-toe with coconuts and driftwood. Pretty
much everybody else was sacked out, too, except for
Jackson—who appeared at the tree line, covered with sweat
and grime, a bundle of something thrown over his shoulder,
his big knife in his hand. Looked like he was trying to cut his
own path into the jungle.

"What is he doing?" Daley asked. "He disappears for
hours at a time."

"How should I know?" Nathan answered, shaking his
wild mane of hair. "It's not like he talks to anybody."

A mischievous smile crept across Daley's face, and
Nathan picked up on it. "Should we?" she asked.

"It's not like we're busy."

They got up and ran couched down, commando-style,
to the edge of the trees. From there it was easy to follow
Jackson's tall figure as he slashed through the underbrush,
carrying his mysterious bundle. *What's up with him?* Daley
wondered.

Jackson finally stopped in a small clearing, so Daley and
Nathan had to sneak up on him. They found good hiding
spots behind a clump of ferns and carefully peeked over
the greenery. When she saw what he was working on, Daley
wished that she had never learned Jackson's secret.

He was making a raft. A totally lame, pathetic little raft.
It was made out of bamboo and vines and was so small and

flimsy that it clearly wouldn't even hold the weight of one person. Well, maybe Lex.

"Oh, *man*," Nathan said, obviously disappointed.

"He's gotta be kidding," Daley whispered. She was having a hard time not laughing out loud—it was the most miserable thing anybody had ever built.

"Is that an escape raft?" Nathan asked.

Despite their best efforts, the two began to snicker.

"You two having fun?" Jackson asked coldly, without even looking at them.

Trying to wipe the grins off their faces, Daley and Nathan stumbled out of the ferns. "Sorry," Nathan said. "Busted."

Daley couldn't keep a straight face. "You can't be serious. I mean, c'mon, a raft?" She walked toward Jackson and inspected his work, but the fragile craft didn't look any safer close-up. "Credit for the effort," she said, "but what do you know about building a boat?"

"Really!" Nathan agreed. "You don't think anybody's gonna sail that thing, do you?"

Daley touched the raft gently, afraid it would fall apart. "Don't worry, it'll sink before it gets deep enough for anyone to drown," she joked. "I suppose we could use it for firewood."

Jackson muscled his way between her and the raft. "I didn't ask for your opinion," he muttered.

Daley gulped and managed a wan smile. "Hey! C'mon! I'm just giving you a hard time—"

"Save it," Jackson muttered.

Nathan jumped between them and stared at the bigger teen. "C'mon, man, lighten up."

"Back off," Jackson growled. He turned to Daley. "You . . . mind your own business."

Daley gaped at him. She was seldom at a loss for words,

but at that moment her mind was a total blank.

"Dude," Nathan said, pulling on Jackson's arm. "Leave her alone!"

Jackson ripped his arm away from Nathan and said, "Don't 'dude' me."

Could Nathan win a fight with Jackson? Was the situation destined to escalate? It didn't really matter. No matter who won a fight on this island, the truth was, everybody would lose. Daley grabbed Nathan and pulled him away from the confrontation.

"Let's just go," she whispered.

Nathan still looked more hurt than angry. "What is your problem?" he called as they walked away.

Jackson didn't respond, only balled his hands into fists, pulled his knife, and walked back into the jungle.

When they were far enough away, Daley turned to Nathan. "What was that? I mean, okay, maybe I was a little harsh about the raft—but the guy just went off."

Nathan nodded somberly and said, "I've been waiting for something like that to happen. Jackson's been a misfit from the second he showed up at school. Back home it didn't matter; here, we've gotta deal. Not good."

Nathan stormed off as if he didn't want to talk to anyone, not even Daley. Would he tell the others? Should *she* tell them? No, they had enough on their minds. If there was going to be a problem with Jackson, they'd find out soon enough.

Lex turned on the video camera, sat down in front of it, and tried not to be nervous. But he was counting on the older kids to follow his lead, and that didn't always work.

Daley would be the key, because if his own sister bagged his idea, the others would ignore him, too.

Lex

Everybody's homesick, and bored. And underneath the boredom, we're all scared. I figure I'll try to do something to get our minds off things. Besides, it's a special day, so I want to have some fun for a change.

Lex turned off the camera and grabbed the camp shovel. Since nobody was working, nobody was using it.

It's a gorgeous sand castle, Taylor thought as she looked at the sumptuous construction she had sculpted on the beach. *More like a sand mansion, someplace in upper Bel Air that all the neighbors will complain about. They'll say it's too big. I'll have a mansion like that someday.*

She looked around nervously.

Either that, or I'll have a bamboo hut and a bunch of coconuts.

With a sigh, Taylor plunged her digging spoon into the sand and surveyed their rustic surroundings. A few people were hanging by the fire pit, and the only one on the beach was Lex. For some time, the kid had been digging trenches in the sand and putting up poles and ropes and vines. He was even using some seats from the airplane and netting from the luggage compartment.

Taylor thought that if she watched long enough, Lex's project would eventually make sense. But it didn't. So she stood up, wiped the sand off her skirt, and strolled toward the busy boy.

The closer she got to the ramshackle formation, the less sense it made. There were holes full of coconuts, hanging nets, stretched ropes, and pretty banners. It looked as if a hard rain could wash it all away.

Taylor crossed her arms and asked, "What exactly are you doing?"

"It's a surprise," he answered as he tied two poles together.

Taylor grumbled, "I hate surprises."

Lex smiled. "Then you're really gonna hate this."

Taylor scowled and walked slowly away from Lex.

Eric couldn't believe his good fortune. All this time with everyone ragging on him, and suddenly he wasn't the scapegoat anymore. His smile broadened as Daley and Nathan told him about their confrontation with Jackson. Eric didn't know which part was funnier—their indignation or Jackson's puny raft.

"All right, we got us a feud!" Eric exclaimed, slapping Nathan on the back. "Thanks, man, things were getting a little stale."

"It's not funny," Nathan protested. "You should have seen him. I thought he was gonna take me apart."

Daley shook her head in disbelief. "All I did was make fun of his raft. Why did he get so angry?"

"I don't know," Nathan snapped. "I don't know anything about the guy."

"Doesn't he come from, like, Compton or someplace nasty like that?" Eric added, hoping to throw some fuel on the fire.

"I heard that, too," Nathan answered. "I tried to talk to him once at school. You know, figured I'd kinda get to know him better? But the guy doesn't say a word. It's useless."

Daley frowned and whispered, "Isn't he living with a foster family?"

"That's the impression I got," Nathan said. "But, like I say, he wasn't exactly a fountain of information."

"What did he do to get taken away from his family?" Daley said.

"I bet they're scared of him, too, huh," Nathan said.

"Oooh, man . . . hostility," Eric hooted. "Nathan, you've got depth."

"Hey, look, my point is just that he's different from us," Nathan said. "People like him have different values. You never know what a guy like that will do." Nathan leaned toward them. "We'd better watch our backs."

Eric lifted his eyes and pointed over Nathan's shoulder. "Uh, Nathan?"

"What?"

"Watch your back." Eric gave him a smile.

Nathan whirled around to see Jackson standing near the tent, glaring at them. It was clear that he had heard their whole conversation. Eric choked back a laugh. *Who says life on a deserted island is boring?*

Jackson stared Nathan down until Nathan finally looked away. Then Jackson tossed some water bottles onto the ground and stomped off, probably to finish his pathetic raft. Daley looked miserable and confused, and Nathan looked as if he had just dodged a charging rhino.

Eric rubbed his hands together. This new soap opera was better than TV.

EIGHTEEN

Melissa had heard the talk about Jackson, even though she tried to stay away from it. She even tried to stay away from her fellow survivors that morning, because they were all acting a little weird. It looked like Lex was digging a network of latrines on the beach, and Daley and Nathan were goofing off and getting into trouble.

Okay, so Jackson had been surly that morning, according to some people. Melissa knew that a scowl came to his face a lot easier than a smile, and silence was his favorite form of expression. "Mysterious" was his middle name. But that didn't make him some kind of dangerous monster.

It's his deeds and leadership we have to respect, not just his words. He's kind of a caveman in that department.

She worried about what would happen if she ever got the courage to tell Jackson how she really felt about him. If he laughed or said, "Fat chance," that would at least be an answer. More likely, he would say nothing and just walk away. Leaving her feeling like a complete and total idiot.

Either way, she was going to find out. Right now. She had hunted him down in his secret clearing.

Melissa slowed her step as she approached, because his behavior looked violent. Jackson was using his big knife like a machete as he sliced and hacked his way through freshly cut branches and bamboo stalks. He worked like a man possessed, stopping only to sharpen his blade on a little whetstone he carried in a pouch on his leather sheath.

His raft is not as lame as they said, Melissa decided. *It's just . . . small. Why did he make it so small? Why has he been working so hard on it?*

She took a deep breath and walked forward. "Wow, it's really coming along."

Jackson said nothing and continued to hack at the bamboo. Sweat streamed from his body. Papery slivers of dead bamboo leaves covered his shoulders and stuck to his hair. With each stroke, a piece of bamboo fell. *Chunk, chunk, chunk.* The bamboo parted with a hollow thud. With a shiver, she realized that a single stroke of that big knife he always carried could probably take off your arm. Not that he would do anything like that, of course! But still. It was kind of amazing just how much damage that knife could do . . . to anything.

He continued slashing away, throwing each fallen stalk of bamboo over his shoulder onto a pile on the ground.

He was stonewalling her. Time for a new tactic—the direct approach. "So what happened?" she asked.

Chunk! Another stalk of bamboo came down, swishing and clattering as it fell. He tossed it over his shoulder without looking, narrowly missing her. *Chunk!* Down came yet another piece of the woody plant.

Melissa smiled. "Don't be angry. I've known Nathan a long time. He's just scared."

"What's he ever had to be scared of?"

Melissa caught her breath. "I mean, about being stuck here and not knowing if we're gonna get rescued or—"

"I know guys like Nathan. Their whole lives they're told how special they are, so they start to believe it."

"And what kind of guy are you?"

Chunk!

"Seriously. I mean, it's easy to say stuff about other people, right? What kind of guy are you?"

Ka-chunk! He nearly cut two pieces of bamboo with one savage chop. He turned to look her in the eye just long enough to speak one short sentence: "The kind that always has to prove it."

Then he turned back and began slashing away at the bamboo. Melissa knew she had been dismissed. Here she was trying to connect with him, and he was so wrapped up in his own little world that he couldn't bring himself to even *look* at her. Not for more than about five seconds, anyway.

"That's it?" she said. "Interview over?"

Chunk! Chunk!

She couldn't believe that he was going to prove anything with that tiny raft, except that they had maybe selected the wrong person as their leader.

There had to be a better explanation for that small raft. A one-man raft could mean only one thing. It hit her like a punch in the stomach.

Jackson is planning to get off the island alone!

Wheeee-oooh! The sound system squealed a high, shrill

piercing noise that cut into your ears like a drill through the head. Lex put his hand over the microphone, cutting off the awful feedback noise.

He had spent the last few minutes patching the mike from Captain Russell's radio headset into the circuit he'd used to amplify the mp3 player. Now he'd be able to project the sound of his voice practically halfway across the island. He didn't want anyone to catch on to his surprise until he announced it himself.

Lex put one leg up onto the wing of the plane, slipped and fell to the sand, almost knocking the breath out of him. The headset flew off. He ignored the pain in his side, retrieved the headset, climbed immediately back up on the wing again, and spoke into the microphone. His amplified voice boomed across the beach: "Attention! Attention! Let the games begin! Step right up, one and all. The competition will soon get underway!" The microphone squealed horribly again. It sounded awful, but, boy, it would sure get everybody's attention.

He turned his head a little so the sound system would stop feeding back.

It worked. He definitely had their attention now! The older kids all slowly rose to their feet and looked in his direction. "Gather 'round. Don't be shy. Everybody . . . everybody!"

Like zombies, the sleepy teenagers plodded over to the plane, looks of confusion on most of their faces. Lex saw all of them but Jackson.

"What's up?" Daley asked.

"I'm announcing the first official—" Taylor pulled the plug of his squeaky microphone out of the amplifier. Now that they were all gathered, he didn't need it anyway. Lex took off the headset and went on without the mike. "I'm announcing the first official Twenty-Nine Down Maze-a-thon!"

"That's not a real word," Eric said with a sneer.

"What are you talking about, Lex?" Nathan asked.

Lex grinned and said, "I say we should have some fun for a change."

"Hel-lo!" Taylor shouted. "I've been saying that since the minute we landed."

"Crashed, you mean?" Daley said.

"Guys! Guys! Focus. You want fun, then follow me!" Lex waved at the older kids and led them around the plane to his elaborate obstacle course, which was dug in the sand the length of the beach.

"Yeah?" Daley asked, sounding impressed but confused. "So what is it?"

"It's an obstacle course," Lex declared. "See, right there, there's a climbing component. You climb over that little wall. Then you crawl under all that string. Kinda like the barbed wire soldiers crawl under in boot camp? Then right there, see, you got hopscotch, hurdles—well, all these little contests. I'll explain each module in a minute."

"Module!" Taylor said. "You're making it sound like some icky test in PE class."

Eric frowned with disappointment. "Anyway, I thought you said it was a maze."

"We'll divide up into two teams and race," Lex announced. The others looked at one another as if such competition was an alien idea. "C'mon! It'll be fun!"

"And . . . what exactly is the fun part?" Taylor asked.

"I know!" Eric crowed. "Winner gets voted off the island."

"Really!" Taylor said. "Then you better believe I'm gonna win! I'm sick of this place."

Everyone laughed.

Taylor looked around, blinking. "What!" she said.

182

"Seriously, though," Lex said, "I thought the winning team would get the rest of the day off from chores," he said, "and the losers would have to be their servants."

There were mutters of approval, and Eric said, "I'd kill for that."

"Why?" Daley asked. "You hardly do anything as it is."

Melissa piped up, "I think it sounds like fun."

"Me too," Daley said. "What are the teams?"

"That's my call," Lex answered. "I was thinking Daley, Taylor, and Nathan against Melissa, Eric, and Jackson. Since I'm the judge, I won't compete. We'll race right after lunch. Is everybody in?"

"Sure. Okay. Why not?" they answered. No one was jumping up and down with excitement, but even Taylor agreed to the contest.

That's a start, Lex thought. *Once we get the game underway, I bet they'll like it. They like most of the stuff I do for them.*

Melissa was excited. She like organized activities. The more organized, the better. Lex was the most industrious of all of them, and he seemed to know what they needed . . . and when they needed it. She could tell that he had really planned this obstacle course, like he planned everything he did. It was going to be fun!

And to think, Daley had almost left him at home. Only Lex's excellent grades in high-school-level courses had gotten him on this field trip. Now it was easy to imagine what trouble they would be in without him.

Fidgeting with excitement, Melissa ticked her fingers as she counted the people gathered on the beach. She frowned. "Wait, what about Jackson?" she asked. "We can't do it without him."

Everyone glanced at Nathan, and he scowled and looked away.

"Yeah, Nathan," Eric said with a mischievous grin. "What about Jackson? Maybe you should ask him if he wants to come out and play."

"I'll get some fruit," Nathan said, moving quickly toward the jungle. "We'll need the energy."

"I'll get some water," Melissa added, taking off after him.

Nathan made fast time down the path, but Melissa had a good idea where he was headed. She caught up with him in a stand of trees where they had just started foraging for food.

"Hey," she said.

"Hey." Nathan jumped up, trying to grab a clump of figs off a high branch. He didn't get them.

Melissa took a deep breath and asked, "What happened with you and Jackson?"

"I don't really know," he answered, reaching again for the figs and grabbing them. "The guy's a loose cannon."

"I don't see it," she answered quickly.

Nathan rolled his eyes. "That's because you didn't see him get all ramped up when we made fun of his goofy raft."

"He's working hard on that," she answered defensively. "You'd be mad, too."

"Not like *that*. I thought he was going to start a fight."

Melissa shook her head. "He wouldn't do that."

"You weren't there," Nathan reminded her. He spotted some fruit on the ground under a tree and picked up a papaya that was still in good shape.

Melissa followed him and asked, "I heard you said some things about him."

"What?" Nathan snapped. "Like he's a mystery guy who comes from a rough part of town, and that he keeps to himself? That's the truth. Like he's different from us? Hey, that happens to be a fact, too."

Melissa shook her head, disgusted. "So just because he doesn't come from the same safe, happy neighborhood as you—where everybody's dad's a lawyer and everybody's mom's a doctor—you think he's strange and dangerous?"

Nathan looked away.

"I saw those ads on TV when your dad was running for district attorney of Los Angeles last year," she continued. "They made a big thing about how he grew up in some sketchy part of L.A. He probably grew up on the same street as Jackson."

"Yeah, and he got out of there the minute he had a chance."

"Which is pretty much what Jackson's doing, wouldn't you say?"

"C'mon, Mel, you're twisting everything around. Why are you making *me* sound like the big jerk here?" Nathan muttered.

Melissa just looked at him, waiting for him to prove her wrong.

"I'm not the one who pulled a knife on somebody."

"That's not exactly the way Daley told it. I mean, he's cutting down bamboo. How's he supposed to do that without having a knife in his hand?"

"You *know* me. I'm not some elitist snob."

"I also know we're all stressed," she answered. "Let's face it. That makes all of us do things we wouldn't normally do."

Nathan shrugged and foraged for more food.

She chased him down and said, "Why don't you go tell Jackson about Lex's competition?"

"Yeah, right. Speaking of things I wouldn't normally do."

"I'm serious," she insisted. "Maybe it'll mend some fences."

"Yeah, or break some bones," Nathan muttered. "Mine."

Melissa kept after him until he finally said, "Why should *I* be the one to make peace? *He* started it."

She took the fruit from his hands and piled it in her shirt. "I think I saw some mangoes where Jackson's making his raft. You might wander over there . . . and just . . . I mean, it can't hurt to *mention* it."

Nathan sighed and strode off into the trees. Melissa understood where he was coming from, but he didn't really know anything about Jackson. None of them did. It was pointless to complain about where Jackson came from because none of that mattered now. *We're all equal on this island.*

Besides, we can't afford to hold grudges in a situation like this—we need each other too much.

While the others were eating lunch and bragging about how they were going to win the race and get servants, Taylor kept an eye on Lex. The kid was dressing up the finish line of his obstacle course with red flowers and green palm fronds. Taylor had never been certain they needed a boy genius on the island, but she had to admit that Lex came up with good ideas.

Unfortunately, this wasn't one of them.

She walked up behind him and said, "And you're doing this because . . . ?"

"Because it's fun."

"Fun?" she asked. "Setting up sticks and coconuts in the sand?"

He grabbed one of his sticks and pushed it deeper into the sand. "Sure. It's fun thinking up the course."

"You are such an odd little boy," Taylor remarked, wrinkling her nose.

"I just want to do something *today* that's a little bit special, that's all."

There was something about the emphasis he put on the word *today* that seemed odd. Taylor crossed her arms and asked, "Really? Why not yesterday? Or tomorrow? The days all seem pretty much the same to me."

"Because I just want to, okay?" Lex snapped.

"Fine, whatever." Taylor threw up her hands and walked away. If Boy Genius wanted to flip out, he was totally welcome to. She glanced back over her shoulder and saw Lex sitting in the sand with a gloomy look on his face.

Maybe he's just going crazy like the rest of us.

Chunk! Chunk! Chunk! From a distance, Nathan watched Jackson methodically hacking at a branch with the knife, and he slowed his approach. *I wish he didn't always have that knife in his hand. Obviously he doesn't love criticism.*

Nathan stood at the edge of the clearing, watching Jackson turn his project over and tie a new stick to its base. The craft looked a bit sturdier than before, but still only big enough for one person . . . who would be sure to drown.

"Spying on me again?" Jackson asked, with eyes in the back of his head.

Nathan cleared his throat nervously and stepped out of the trees. "I came to clear the air." Jackson kept right on working, so Nathan kept on talking. "I said some things I didn't mean."

"So you don't think that you're better than me?" Jackson asked coldly.

"Did I ever say that?" Nathan said.

"You said that I didn't belong at your school because I come from a totally different world."

"No, what I said is—" Nathan broke off in the middle of the sentence. There was no way to get out of this looking good. Pretty much no matter how you said it, Jackson had a right to feel insulted.

"Go on," Jackson said. "I'm real interested to hear this."

"Look, I don't want to fight with you," Nathan said. "I came to tell you that Lex built this obstacle course, and he wants to have a relay race."

Jackson looked at him like it was about the dumbest idea he'd ever heard in his life.

"Hey, I know, I know," Nathan said. "It's just kid stuff. But the guy's ten years old. Why don't you humor him? He went through a lot of trouble."

Jackson whaled on the branch some more. Wood chips flew left and right.

"Anyway, there's gonna be two teams. Lex will be the referee. So if you're not there, the teams will be uneven."

Jackson didn't say anything. But at least he'd stopped swinging the big knife.

"C'mon. What's the problem? It'll be fun. The way the game's gonna work, the team that wins gets to have the other team be their servants."

Jackson tested the sharpness of the knife with his thumb, then stabbed it down into the branch, impaling it deep into the wood. He lifted one eyebrow. "Servants? For how long?"

"A day, I guess?"

"And what are the teams?"

Nathan counted them off. "Well, let's see. It's me and

Daley and Taylor—against Melissa, Eric—"

"—and me." Jackson finished his sentence. Then shrugged. "I mean . . . *if* I decide to play."

"Right."

"So you and me are on opposite teams?"

Nathan nodded.

Jackson gave him an ominous smile. "Tell Lex I'll be there." He pried his blade out of the branch.

"Cool." Nathan tried to make it sound like he didn't really care one way or the other. But for some reason he actually felt kind of glad that Jackson would be competing in Lex's silly little contest.

He had started walking away when Jackson called after him. "Hey, Nathan. Start practicing your table-waiting skills."

"Huh?"

Jackson had a thin smile on his face. "'Cause you're gonna be serving my food all day."

Nathan grinned. "Don't count on it."

NINETEEN

et's see, Nathan thought, *I nearly killed myself trying to climb a coconut tree when the jungle is littered with fruit. I got a rash so bad downstairs that I had to wear Taylor's skirt. I destroyed the signal kite and wasted a flare. Don't forget, I blew the chance to be our leader by pushing too hard and feuding with Daley.*

Of course, that was nothing compared to the feud he was having with Jackson. Nathan had never expected Daley to punch him out—except with words—but Jackson was a different case. And there were no adults around to break them up.

And here we thought life on the island couldn't get any worse, Nathan thought.

Lex was talking in his announcer voice, so Nathan decided to snap out of it and listen. The two teams were arrayed side by side at the starting line of the obstacle course, which ran down the beach and back. Nathan, Daley, and Taylor were on one side, with Eric, Melissa, and Jackson on the other. Lex was standing between the two teams.

"Here's the main rule," Lex announced. "You've got to run the course four times, which means one person from each team has to run it twice. Who's it gonna be?"

Nathan's stomach got queasy, because he realized that he was the only boy on his team. Daley was really competitive and would knock herself out to win, but she didn't exactly rush out to volunteer for the extra lap.

Jackson waved and stepped forward.

"Okay, Jackson from his team!" Lex announced. "And?"

Nathan played football and ran track—so he was the natural one to do the extra lap. But he was a little intimidated by Jackson. What if Nathan won and Jackson got all gangster on him and came after him with a knife? That wouldn't be very cool, either. While he was thinking about it, someone else stepped forward.

Taylor, of all people!

"I'll do it," Taylor said brightly, flipping her long hair over one shoulder, then striking a muscleman pose.

Everyone on both teams looked shocked.

Melissa blurted out, "Really?"

"Me?" Taylor laughed loudly. "Get serious. Of course not!" She stepped back, then prodded Nathan in the ribs. "Come on, jock boy."

Nathan didn't really have much of a choice.

He stumbled forward and joined Jackson at the starting line. It was also the finish line, which meant that Nathan would have to run it four times, down and back, racing against Jackson each leg.

Awesome, he thought. *Just perfect.*

"Okay, Nathan and Jackson run the first and last legs!" Lex proclaimed.

"Can I talk with my team for a second?" Nathan asked. "We need to strategize."

"Sure," Lex agreed. "Huddle time!"

In their huddle, Daley took over. "I think I should race against Eric," she whispered. "I know I can pick up some time on him. He's such a wuss, I know that if I can get out in front of him at the beginning, he'll just give up. Taylor, you can hold your own against Melissa, right?"

The blonde shrugged. "How should I know? But I'll tell you this, I don't intend to be serving mango frappes to *her* all afternoon. Plus, if we lose, Eric will be bugging me all day to massage his back. Not happening."

"Me either!" Daley said.

Taylor looked at her like, *I don't think that's very likely.* But fortunately she didn't say anything.

"Okay," Nathan said, taking a deep breath. "Are you sure neither one of you wants to go first and last?"

Taylor wrinkled her nose. "You're not *scared* of him are you?"

"Well . . . no, of course not. It's just I got a little bit out-of-shape since the end of the season and—"

"Shut up and get out there." Taylor pushed him sharply.

Nathan nodded and shook his arms, loosening up a little. Then he walked back to the starting line where Jackson was waiting for him, grim-faced. *It's just possible that I might be faster than him*, Nathan thought. *Yeah, he's big and hard-looking, but that doesn't mean he's got wheels.*

"Take your marks!" Lex ordered, and the two boys got down in their best racing crouches. "This is for the Twenty-Nine Down Maze-a-thon world championship!"

"It's not a maze!" Eric said for about the fourth time.

"Whatever," Lex said, undaunted. "Winners have no chores for the rest of the day; losers are their servants."

"Ready?" Lex held up his hand, and Nathan tensed, determined to get a good start. "Set . . . *go!*"

Nathan bolted from the line and didn't look back until he got to the first obstacle—the trench crawl. He dove under the tangle of ropes and strings, then wriggled like a worm through the sand. As he neared the end of the trench, he glanced back. Jackson was about ten feet behind, just getting started with the trench. He seemed to have snagged his belt on one of the ropes and was having trouble getting free.

I'm gonna win this leg, Nathan thought with excitement. He crawled even faster, cleared the ropes, and lunged to his feet—just in time to jump the mini-hurdles. A glance behind him showed that Jackson was slipping even farther back, although his long legs made jumping the hurdles easy.

Nathan finished that obstacle and got to the fence, which was about six feet tall. He climbed it with ease and slid down the other side. *I still have a comfortable lead.* Lex was shouting into his microphone, but it was hard to hear with so much blood pumping in Nathan's ears.

He skipped through a hopscotch pattern, then had to stop to transfer coconuts from one hole to another. Here Nathan lost a few seconds, but he still finished before Jackson even got there. Nathan dashed across the sand and slid under the limbo sticks, and he heard the other team yelling at Jackson to hurry.

I'm gonna beat him for sure!

Next came the most difficult obstacle—a balance beam only about two inches wide. Nathan had never been a gymnast, but he skittered along the beam as fast as he could. Lex had said that anyone who fell off had to start over. Nathan felt himself wobble a couple of times, but by flailing his arms and charging ahead at maximum speed, he managed to clear the obstacle before he fell over sideways. He somersaulted, then sprang to his feet.

I'm almost done! All I have to do is round the pole at the end of the course and head for home!

Behind him Jackson was slogging along, falling farther back, but Nathan never slowed down for a moment. He could see Taylor preparing to run, and he knew they might need all the extra seconds they could get.

The return leg was straight running along the length of the course—on the sand between the two tracks. There was no doubt that Nathan was going to win, but running in sand was tiring. The soles of his feet hurt from digging in to get traction. He was exhausted by the time he reached the finish line and slapped Taylor's hand.

Nathan collapsed in the sand, panting, and watched Jackson finish up the course. The bigger kid wasn't even breathing heavily, and he was smiling. Which made Nathan a little nervous. Had Jackson been pacing himself? Or was he going slowly just to make things interesting later on? Nathan put it out of his mind and switched his attention to the race.

Melissa took off like a linebacker chasing a quarterback, but Nathan felt good about giving Taylor such a big lead.

When he heard Daley groan, Nathan turned to watch his teammate's progress. The first thing he saw was that Taylor was running in her flip-flops.

"What is she *thinking*?" Nathan said.

Daley just shook her head.

Taylor was following the course but making miserable time. The trench crawl went badly. She got caught on a rope and instead of pushing ahead, she looked back helplessly at Daley and Nathan. Melissa got stuck once, too, but just bulled ahead, pulling herself free and evening up the race.

When they reached the hurdles, Taylor really fell apart. She got her feet tangled, tripped, and stumbled through the vines. With a pout, Taylor tried to detour around the hurdles, but Lex warned her to finish every obstacle. She started to argue with Lex.

"Just *go!*" shouted Daley.

Nathan waved his arms in a big circle, signaling her to shut her mouth and just keep going. Taylor stamped her foot, then muddled over the hurdles.

Melissa, meanwhile, was way ahead, and she handled every challenge with ease. It wasn't that she was all that athletic. It was just that she was completely focused. She had an expression of determination that kind of surprised Nathan. Usually she would kick herself every time she made a mistake. But now?

"Man," Nathan said, "look at Melissa. It's like total eye of the tiger."

"I am so gonna kill Taylor," Daley said.

"Look," Nathan said, "just get even with Eric and I'll take it home in the stretch."

Daley nodded tensely. He could see her getting revved up, figuring out exactly how she was going to approach each obstacle. He decided to stop talking and let her concentrate.

Taylor plodded along in her flip-flops, and Lex pretty much gave up trying to keep her on course. She did only about half the balance beam before she turned and staggered back to the finish line.

After Melissa's tag, Eric got off to a great head start on Daley. But he thought he already had the race won. He jogged goofily, raising his hands in the air like he was taking a victory lap.

Daley waited with gritted teeth for Taylor to finally slap her hand.

When the redhead took off, she tore off down the beach, sand spraying up from her running shoes. She caught Eric during the crawl, and she passed him when they climbed over the fence. Eric's eyes widened as he saw her pulling even with him under the ropes. Suddenly Eric's comedy act was over. He was trying as hard as he could.

But it was too little too late. Just like Taylor, he had frittered away a lead, and he was never going to catch a determined Daley. There had been too many cheeseburgers, too much time in front of the TV, too little exercise for him to catch up with her.

By the time Daley finished and handed off to Nathan, their team was ahead by several seconds. Nathan figured he could beat Jackson the same way he had beat him on the first leg.

But this was a different Jackson.

The big guy caught Nathan in the trench crawl, and he swam through the sand like it was water. Nathan was panting for all he was worth, but he was still tired from the first leg of the race. He lost the lead at the fence climb, and he realized that Jackson had saved his energy to go all-out in the final leg.

It was all a blur after that. Everything that could go wrong for Nathan did. It wasn't that he was uncoordinated so much as he was trying too hard. His aching limbs and burning lungs just couldn't keep up with what he tried to tell them to do. He fell in the hurdles, had to take two runs at the wall, and then fell off the balance beam three times in a row.

Jackson, on the other hand, barely seemed to notice the hurdles, his long legs powering over them. He blazed through the hopscotch like a pro halfback doing agility drills, and slid under the limbo stick in one smooth swoop. Nathan felt like his arms would fall off when he transferred the coconuts from one hole to another, and he felt like a total loser. *I've lost the match for us. I let that caveman beat me!*

Jackson was twenty feet ahead when he reached the pole at the end of the course. Instead of running back the other way, he paused and waited for Nathan to catch up.

"What are you doing?" Eric screamed with alarm.

"Run! C'mon!" Melissa cried, shaking her fists.

Nathan's jaw was drooping, and his tongue hung out. He was wheezing by the time he reached Jackson. Jackson looked at him and smiled. "You never know what guys like me are gonna do."

Jackson began to take off his tennis shoes. Nathan wasn't going to wait around and watch him. Although his muscles were screaming and his lungs were bursting, Nathan took off as fast as he could for the finish line.

Everyone was screaming now, and Lex was squealing as loud as the sound system. The sand felt muddy and thick. It bogged Nathan down. He didn't need to look behind him to see Jackson, because he could hear the big guy panting down his neck.

I'm there! I can almost touch the finish line . . . any moment now! But, kicking sand like a dune buggy, Jackson flew by him and crossed the line just a second before Nathan did.

"Woo-hoo! Yeah! All right!" the victors screamed. Taylor pouted. Daley turned away, muttering angrily. Lex announced the winners, as if anybody needed to hear it officially.

The winners considered what to do with their new servants. Jackson flashed Nathan a smile, but Nathan turned away. He wasn't going to forgive and forget that easily.

I'm gonna steer clear of him, Nathan decided. *Maybe that way I can avoid having to do anything for him.*

TWENTY

O kay, that was fun, Daley thought. But it would have been a lot more fun if my stupid team had won.

She swallowed her competitive drive and congratulated the winners. They weren't being too smug about it. Yet. Lex accepted everyone's compliments for designing and building the obstacle course, then disappeared. Jackson and Melissa she could probably deal with. But if the day ended before she was forced to drown Eric in the ocean, it would be a very big surprise to her.

Daley found her little brother near the plane, hammering a metal strip onto something. When she looked over his shoulder, she was surprised to see that he had made a large distress sign that read, "SOS. WE'RE ALIVE. 29 DWN."

"Hey, looking good!" she told him.

Lex nodded. "When a plane goes over, it might catch a reflection off the letters."

"That's awesome," Daley said, really meaning it. "Hey,

the race was fun. What made you think of it?"

The boy shrugged. "Oh, I don't know. I wanted to make today a little special."

"How come?"

"I just thought we needed it," Lex said, looking expectantly at her.

Daley thought he wanted to do their family knuckle handshake, so she held out her fist. Lex responded halfheartedly, and for the first time she realized that something was wrong. He looked at the ground, and Daley didn't know what to say. Since she had goofed off all day, she wanted to do some work before the winners gave her a really nasty chore to do.

She walked away, taking one more glance over her shoulder. Her brother was not his usual upbeat self, even though his maze-a-thon had been a success-a-thon. It was odd. He wasn't the moody type.

Well, he did make that distress sign. Lex is really worried about not getting rescued. Sure, we all are. But he's the only one on this island who is ten years old. If we have to spend a long time here . . .

Well, she didn't want to think about that.

"Beautiful day at the club, isn't it?" Eric asked.

"Quite so," Melissa replied.

Eric and Melissa were lounging on airplane seats in the shade from the canopy, sipping drinks in coconut shells with little umbrellas. Finally—being stranded on a desert island was feeling ever-so-slightly like vacation.

Eric turned to her, doing his best imitation of a rich jerk. Which, actually, was not that hard for him to pull off. "Say, my dear, would you perhaps care for another delicious and refreshing beverage?"

"Why, yes," Melissa replied. "That would be lovely."

Eric nodded and snapped his fingers loudly. Several times. "Young lady! We need to be replenished!"

Taylor shuffled over, glowering at the two winners, and splashed some water from a bottle into their coconuts. She stood sighing loudly as Eric went through his performance for the tenth time—swishing the drink in the air, then taking a long sip, sloshing it around in his mouth like he was tasting wine at some nice restaurant.

"Why, thank you, kind fräulein!" Eric said enthusiastically. He pointed to the umbrella above them. "Would you mind adjusting the shade? I must be frank with you, my dear, I'm feeling just . . ." He held his finger and thumb about a millimeter apart. ". . . just the tiniest trifle warm."

"You're gonna feel my foot kicking your head if you keep this up," Taylor snapped.

"Now, now!" Eric said with mock horror. "Is that any way for a servant to speak?"

Taylor stomped her foot and muttered, "I am so going to kill Lex."

"Yes, yes, of course, my dear," he said. "But I must insist that you wait until after you've given me my back rub."

Instead of answering him, she accidentally-on-purpose squirted him with water. When she was done, it looked like he'd peed in his pants.

"I think you had a little accident," she said. *"Sir."*

Then she stomped away, hips swinging.

Eric watched until she had disappeared around the other side of the plane. He shook his head sadly. "It is *so* hard to find good help these days."

"Sad but true, my friend," Melissa said. "Sad but true."

They raised their coconuts and clicked them together in a silent toast. Then they started giggling.

Nathan and Daley were hauling well water when Jackson cornered both of them at the fire pit.

"Yeah?" Nathan asked, grabbing an empty jug to head back.

Jackson smiled and said, "I'm here to collect my winnings. Come with me." He crooked his finger and strode off into the jungle.

Nathan and Daley looked glumly at each other, dropped the water jugs, and reluctantly followed Jackson into the unknown. Nathan's heart sank as he realized where they were going: the clearing where Jackson was working on his raft. Such a dead-end project.

"If I'm gonna get this done today," Jackson said somberly, "I need your help."

"You want our help?" Daley asked with surprise.

He nodded. "That was the deal, wasn't it? Losing team has to do what the winners say."

Nathan looked at Daley, hoping she'd have some idea about how to avoid wasting their time on this futile project. Daley gave him a helpless shrug. So Nathan held up his hands in surrender and said, "Hey, fine, show us what to do."

After a critical inspection, they nearly tore apart the raft that Jackson had already built. It really took at least two people to keep enough tension to tie the knots properly. The joints would have to be solid to survive a beating at sea. If it ever got that far.

Nathan knew a lot about knots from his Scout days

and from studying the book written by his great-great-grandfather, the famous explorer. Nathan felt better: At least he was able to teach Jackson a few tricks.

The boys cut more bamboo and lashed the stalks together. That was smart—bamboo was stronger and lighter than wood. And it had natural air pockets for buoyancy. Daley wove the vines and made better ropes than Jackson had, and she also added cross supports for stability. Nathan figured out how to add a rudder made from the tail section of the plane. Nathan was a little amazed: Jackson actually complimented him for this addition to the little craft they were building.

By the end of the day, the raft was done. Eight feet long on each side, it was still a miniature version of what they would really need. *Maybe we can use it as a model*, Nathan thought, *or as a way to test raft design*.

Jackson looked at it for a long time, then smiled slightly and nodded once, like this was exactly what he'd wanted to make. Nathan felt a little strange about it. Whatever you wanted to say about the guy—he didn't seem like an idiot. But this raft just didn't seem like it would hack it. Daley was obviously thinking the same thing: She walked up to the raft and gave it a good shake. Her smile slowly faded to a worried frown.

"I know you don't want to hear it," she said, "but I still think it's suicide to take off on this."

"Who said I was going to?" Jackson asked with a half smile.

Nathan blinked with confusion and shook his head. "Uh, well, Daley and I sure aren't gonna use it. And I can pretty much guarantee Eric or Taylor won't be shoving off. That leaves Melissa and—"

"And I'm not letting my brother anywhere near it," Daley

said, giving Jackson a protective glare.

Jackson tested one of the corner joints and said, "Too bad, because it's for him."

"Over my dead body!" Daley shouted.

Nathan gaped at him. "Are you serious? Do you really want Lex or one of us to float off on this thing?"

"Lex doesn't know anything about it," Jackson answered.

"I am so lost," Daley said with frustration. "What do you mean?"

Jackson looked serious when he answered, "While the rest of us are all stressed about who's gonna be in charge and what the other guy's thinking, Lex has been thinking about things that are a little more important."

"Yeah," Nathan agreed. "He's making that sign from scraps. It's a good idea."

"It is," Jackson said. "But seriously, nobody's gonna see it unless we put it out there."

"Put Lex's sign on the raft and send it off?" Nathan asked. He felt like hitting himself with a hammer when he finally realized what all of this was about. "It will be like a message in a bottle!"

"Jackson, that's brilliant," Daley admitted.

"But Lex doesn't know?" Nathan asked, putting together the final piece of the puzzle.

The big guy whispered, "It's a surprise. That's why I needed it done today."

Daley frowned. "What's so important about today?"

Jackson stared at her for a long time. "You're joking, right?" he said finally.

"What?"

"Uh . . . Isn't today his birthday?"

Daley looked as if he had punched her in the stomach.

Nathan had never seen her so stunned and sad all at once. He wanted to comfort her, but what could he say? Missing your own brother's birthday was really kinda not cool.

"That's what he told me on the plane," Jackson added. "I mean, I have the right day, don't I?"

"Yeah," Daley answered glumly. "You're more on top of it than me. I've got a great little brother, and he's got a crummy big sister."

Daley found Lex sitting on a log, tending the constant flame in the fire pit. They could do a lot of foolish things, but they couldn't let the fire go out. Night or day, someone was always tending it, and often more than one person was hanging around. She glanced at the woodpile and realized that they were getting low. Tomorrow it would be back to work, collecting more wood . . . from places farther and farther away.

You can't take a day off from anything in this place. I took a day off from paying attention to my little brother, and I screwed up, big-time. I'll make it up to him. Every day, from here on out.

Lex still looked down. Daley was quiet as she sat beside him on the log.

"Hey," she said.

"Hi."

Daley managed a smile. "So, uh, being stuck here is kind of weird."

"You think?" They both had to laugh at that lame opening line. What an understatement.

"What I mean is," she began, "we're all so far from

normal here that it's hard to remember what normal is."

"Yeah," Lex agreed.

"But you're doing the most to keep us going. That maze-a-thon was brilliant, Lex. It really was. Even Taylor thought so, though she'll never admit it."

His expression brightened. "Really?"

"Yeah. You may be the youngest of us, but you're our heart. While everybody else is off in their own universe, you're keeping us together. You do stuff that keeps us civilized. Human. That makes me feel even worse that I forgot it was your birthday."

Lex's chin trembled, and for the first time since they crashed, Daley thought she saw a tear in his eye. She was so proud of him . . . and so lucky to have him here.

"It's okay, I know there's a lot going on," he finally said.

Daley shook her head and said tearfully, "Yeah, but we have to remember who we are. Happy birthday, Lex."

They gave each other a warm hug, and she said, "I love you."

"I love you, too."

After wiping a tear from her eye, Daley added, "But not everybody is a loser like me. Somebody remembered."

"Who?" Lex sat up at attention.

Daley turned toward the trees and yelled, "Come on in!"

A chant of "Happy birthday!" echoed from the jungle, and the leaves parted to reveal Melissa and the three boys, carrying Jackson's raft. Taylor was perched on top of the raft, waving grandly, like some displaced homecoming queen.

Lex's grin got bigger and bigger, especially when Taylor went to him, took off her flower lei, and draped it around his neck. Then she gave Lex a kiss on the top of his head, and he blushed.

"Jackson has a surprise for you," Daley said.

The big guy smiled and said, "Lex, this is for you, buddy. It may have been my idea, but it couldn't have happened without Nathan and Daley."

Lex gave Daley another hug, and she almost started crying again.

Jackson continued, "I mean, you're always coming up with ideas to make things a little better for us. For a change, this is something that takes one of your ideas and makes it a little better."

He waved to the others, and they stood the raft on one end to reveal Lex's sign, "SOS. WE'RE ALIVE. 29 DWN," lashed securely to the middle.

"It's perfect!" Lex shouted. He was grinning like a bobble-head doll.

"Happy birthday, buddy," Jackson said, and they all gathered around the kid, wishing him well on his special day. Daley could only marvel at this spontaneous outburst of appreciation, even love, for her little brother. But Lex gave a lot, without asking much in return.

He deserved it.

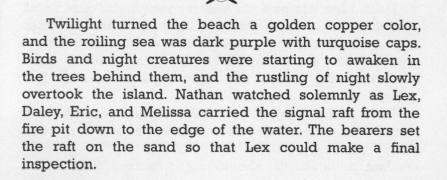

Twilight turned the beach a golden copper color, and the roiling sea was dark purple with turquoise caps. Birds and night creatures were starting to awaken in the trees behind them, and the rustling of night slowly overtook the island. Nathan watched solemnly as Lex, Daley, Eric, and Melissa carried the signal raft from the fire pit down to the edge of the water. The bearers set the raft on the sand so that Lex could make a final inspection.

There was something about launching the raft that made it feel like an important ceremony. Their message in a bottle was a plea for help, and it seemed kind of desperate. But it was also an important statement that they were not going to give up. *We aren't just going to accept our fate and do nothing.*

Nathan felt a presence, and he turned to find Jackson standing beside him. There was a lot he could have said, but Jackson showed that you didn't have to blurt everything you felt. You let your actions do the talking.

However, something still puzzled Nathan. "When exactly did Lex tell you it was his birthday?"

"He told me on the plane," Jackson answered. "He said he was all excited about having a big adventure on his birthday. I guess he got more than he asked for."

Nathan laughed softly. "Yeah, no kidding. Hey, you did a good thing."

Jackson shrugged and looked humble. "Yeah, well, you never know what guys like me are gonna do."

Nathan laughed and said, "If we stay on this island long enough, there won't be much we don't know about each other."

"Yeah," Jackson agreed. His smile faded just a little.

Finally, Lex finished his final inspection of the raft and gave them a thumbs-up. Everyone grabbed a handle on the small craft and carried it into the sea, letting the cool, salty water splash them. With a lot of whooping and hollering, they pushed the raft over a wave, and it cleared the first line of breakers with no problem.

While Taylor hugged Lex and the others cheered, Nathan watched solemnly as the tide carried their hopes into the vast purple beyond.

Nathan felt as if he should talk to Jackson, but Jackson

didn't like to talk. So Nathan took out the video camera and added something to his diary.

Nathan

I'm not gonna say that I'm a jerk, and that I misjudged Jackson. That's too easy. We come from different places, and that makes us different. Not better or worse, just different. But what he did today was pretty cool, and I'm glad that I helped.

Daley

A lot's happened on this trip, and there's more to come. Forgetting my brother's birthday was . . . well, exactly the kind of thing we can't do. If we're going to survive, we've got to keep our humanity, and remember who we are. Like Jackson did. And Lex.

Daley turned off the video camera and the flashlight she was using for light. Sitting in the mouth of the girls' tent, she looked at the fading rays of daylight and wondered how they could keep it together. Boredom, laziness, revenge. Nasty jokes and selfish tantrums . . . none of that would get it done.

Nobody's perfect, but we still have to respect one another. When it really counts, this group can pull together. These seven people are a team, whether we like it or not. We're a family, even if we don't know it yet.

uncharacteristic. Jackson couldn't quite put his finger on what it was. It was like she'd been caught off guard somehow.

The earring looked suspiciously like the fishhooks that Jackson's "friend" had left him.

Taylor couldn't be the mystery friend, though. That was impossible. She was the one person Jackson had absolutely ruled out from the very beginning.

On the other hand, he had been going over and over something in his mind. Somebody had to have been alone with the first-aid kit to leave the note there without being noticed. And he'd narrowed it down to—

"Daley said you had a couple of pairs of earrings," Lex added. "I hope you didn't lose the other ones."

"No," she said lightly. "I know where the others are. Thanks."

Lex turned back to Jackson and said, "Whoa! Look at that butterfly." He pointed at a large yellow insect flitting in the jungle. "You mind if I go catch that for my collection?"

"Knock yourself out," Jackson said.

The boy nodded and ran off. Jackson stared at Taylor, feeling a little dumbfounded.

"It was you," he said finally. "It was you all along."

"Huh?" she said. She looked at him with her usual vacant stare, like nothing was going on in her head at all.

"I went over it and over it in my mind," Jackson said. She had been the only one who had been alone with the first-aid kit after he'd looked at it in the tent. He'd gone back outside, dropped it in the sand. Then everybody had come back into the tent. Everybody except Taylor, who was off having her hissy fit. Or . . . was she? Then Lex had gone back out and gotten the first-aid kit. "It has to be you, Taylor."

EPILOGUE

Lex and Jackson were splitting firewood. Lex wa telling Jackson about his butterfly collection i mind-numbing detail. Jackson mostly just nodded.

While they were working, Taylor sashayed by, hip swinging, carrying a bottle of suntan lotion and a towe She paused, studied the beach carefully as though trying t decide on the perfect location for sunbathing.

Lex looked up and spotted her. "Oh! I almost forgot," h said. "Hey, Taylor!"

Taylor frowned, apparently irritated that he concentration had been broken. "What?"

Lex reached into his pocket and pulled out a shiny silve hoop. "I found this earring in our tent. I don't know how i got there."

He handed her the bauble. Taylor looked embarrassed for a moment. She glanced at Jackson, then looked away quickly. Something flashed in her eyes that seemed

For a minute she stared blankly back at him. Then a brief, sly smile came across her face. She held one finger up to her lips and said:

"Shhhhhhhhhh."

Turn the page for a sneak preview of

#3 The Return

available soon!

ONE

Stupid! Stupid! Stupid! That's the last time I blurt out my feelings in front of a camera. And the last time I even think about a boy!

Melissa stomped through the jungle, wiping tears from her eyes and crushing all the plant and animal life that was unlucky enough to get in her way. After a moment, she got back onto a narrow path—it looked too narrow for humans—and tried to concentrate on the beauty around her. *I'm just taking a walk,* she told herself, *not running away from total humiliation and embarrassment.*

An image of Jackson flashed through her mind, and she rejected it. Just like he had rejected her. Take away the anger and the hurt—and the worst part of it was the disappointment. How could Taylor sink that low? Melissa wanted to run off to some other part of this stupid island and become a hermit. But that would be admitting she was a coward!

Best to keep walking ... to clear my head. To get away from them all. Beautiful day, huh? I'm on an adventure.

After a while, Melissa's forced march through the jungle helped her burn off some of the anger. The others were innocent bystanders ... except for Taylor and Eric, who couldn't be forgiven so easily. Taylor had broadcast Melissa's deepest thoughts for the whole world to hear. For now, the whole world was seven confused kids lost on a tropical island. That was the worst part, because everything was magnified—bigger than life. Wilder, scarier.

From the burn in her thighs and calves, Melissa realized that she had been hiking uphill for some time. She thought about turning back, but she didn't want to see any of them. Yet. Besides, the thick foliage had given way to low ferns and grasses, and the views ahead of her were incredible. Lush, green canyons and jagged mountains with silver waterfalls beckoned her to take a closer look.

I bet no one has ever been here before. Why doesn't somebody build a resort on this island, where we can all go to be pampered? I don't think there's a prettier place on Earth. Maybe that's the whole point—if people were here, it wouldn't be so pretty.

Feeling calm at last, Melissa wandered toward the incredible vista ... a miniature, greener Grand Canyon. She had to stop when she ran out of ground, and she realized that she wasn't going any farther in this direction. Maybe it was time to turn back.

She caught her breath at the wondrous view from the highest point of a bluff, overlooking a vast canyon full of lush greenery. Shimmering waterfalls spread like ribbons through the gullies, and the ground was still damp from a recent rain. *It probably sprinkles every day at this altitude,* Melissa thought, *and it still feels damp.* She bent down to wipe the mud off her boot and could smell the yellow flowers growing in the crevices below her.

Just incredible, Melissa thought. It was worth getting embarrassed and driven insane to see this. The more she gazed at the majestic sight, the more trivial her love life—or lack of—became.

We survived a crash in the Pacific Ocean, and we're surviving being stranded on a deserted island. We're entitled to go a little crazy! What was that quote from Robert Louis Stevenson, who wrote *Treasure Island*? It went something like: When you're home you want to be on an adventure, but when you're on an adventure all you really want is to be home.

That's the stage we've reached, all right. But we have to be proud of ourselves for all the ways we've adapted since the crash. It's either that or perish. Melissa wondered about Captain Russell, Ian, Abby, and Jory—the ones who had gone off to look for help. Had they adapted to life on the march? Or had they done the other thing . . . perish?

We might never know.

Her thoughts turned back to Jackson, and she wanted to slap herself. Her timing had been all wrong. Jackson had a lot to deal with since they elected him leader, and he didn't need to add romance to the list. Being alive, being healthy—that should be enough under these conditions.

Suddenly, Melissa wanted to celebrate being alive, even if she was alone and far from camp. *But I'm not all alone,* she mused, *not with this unspoiled view in front of me . . . and the birds and the flowers.* Melissa pulled off her jacket and stripped down to her shirt, then she lifted her arms to the heavens and stretched. The breeze on that peak felt wonderful and so cleansing.

Squish! Slurp! While she was busy celebrating, Melissa's

heels slipped in the mud, and she fell backward. *"Ulp!"* she blurted as she landed on her rump. When her legs began to slide off the bluff, panic gripped Melissa. She clawed at the ground and came up with . . . blades of grass . . . mud . . . a broken root! Everything crumbled away in her hands, just like the edge of the cliff crumbled beneath her twisting body.

She writhed and screamed, but gravity had her in its clutches, dragging her down . . . down . . . down. Like a kid on a waterslide, Melissa flew off the edge into open space! She twisted onto her stomach and lunged at a rock, but it broke off in her bloody hand. Hope was gone. The vast canyon yawned beneath her feet, and Melissa could do nothing to stop her fall.

Then she crashed back to earth. Rocks bruised her, dirt filled her mouth and nose, but Melissa never stopped clawing to get a handhold. Her feet hit something solid before her hands did, and she slumped against the edge of the cliff. Panting for breath, she curled into a shivering ball, waiting to see what would happen next. Death was still tugging at her sleeve.

Finally she realized she wasn't going to fall any farther. At least not right away. So Melissa pried her eyes open long enough to take a trembling look around. Holding her breath, she stole a glance downward and discovered that she was stuck on a narrow ledge some twenty or thirty feet below the bluff. She was bruised and bleeding but still in one piece. One very endangered piece.

Cautiously, Melissa peered over the edge to discover that it was still a long way to the bottom, with lots of bushes and rocks along the way. For sure, if she had missed this ledge, death was the next stop. The churning in her stomach would not go away, and she almost felt like puking. At least all these panicked reactions told her she was still alive. She still had a chance.

That was until she looked around again and realized how much trouble she was in. Cut off from people who were themselves cut off. "Oh, man," she muttered. "Help!"

Surprise! No answer came. There was no one around to hear her, except for maybe a few exotic birds cruising the canyon's warm air currents. Her bruises, cuts, and aches began to assert themselves, reminding her of all the bounces she had taken on the way down. But she had survived the fall, and that was the least of her worries. Dehydration, cold, exposure, hunger. There was a lot to keeping a human being alive, and she had none of it.

"Help!" she cried again.

Yeah, right. Help. Melissa didn't even know how far she had walked, or in what direction she had gone. Nobody knew. The others probably thought she wanted to be left alone, so they wouldn't come looking for her until much later. Even then, there was no guarantee they would find her.

Out of sight, out of mind.

This wasn't the first time that death seemed like part of the crew. There was the airplane crash itself. That was a doozy. Then Nathan had almost killed himself trying to climb that palm tree. And Eric had almost died from anaphylactic shock, due to eating oysters. Amid all the eye candy on this island, it was easy to forget that death was a big part of the scenery.

"Help!" Melissa yelled again, much louder than before. The breeze gently shushed her, as if saying there was no point in yelling. The vast canyon would swallow every noise she could make. Overhead a bird hooted, and it seemed to be laughing at her plight.

I'm stuck down here, Melissa decided. *I need a miracle.*

Only yesterday, a miracle seemed to be close at hand. After more than a week of struggle, the survivors finally had enough food, water, and shelter to really survive. Last night they had launched a raft with a big SOS sign on it. That was their "message in a bottle" to the outside world. Thanks to Lex, they'd even had some fun racing through his crazy obstacle course.

The band of survivors had begun to respect one another. They didn't take every failure or mistake personally. Where one of them lacked skills and smarts, another one had them. They were on a deserted island, but they were living in each other's pockets. More dependent on one another than they ever thought they could be.

That was yesterday, Melissa thought. *Today is a different animal.*

It all started when Melissa woke up wearing one of Taylor's tops, which she had grabbed in the middle of the night from the floor of the girls' tent. She hadn't realized it was Taylor's button-down lime shirt until the morning. By then, it was too late. By then, she had gotten it dirty. *First mistake.*

No problem, Melissa thought. *I'll just wash it and dry it before Taylor gets up. She always sleeps as late as possible.* Since the sun hadn't risen yet, Melissa couldn't hang the shirt on the line to dry, so she hung it over the fire.

Second mistake, Melissa thought, *and that was the big one.* The fire singed the shirttails of Taylor's precious little top, so there wasn't anything to do but tell Taylor what had happened. *Third mistake.*

Taylor had flipped. "I can't believe you did this! What

were you thinking? This is *my* top!"

"I'm sorry, I'm sorry, I'm sorry," Melissa had said a dozen times, but it had no impact on the preppy cheerleader.

"I have to talk to Jackson about this!" Taylor declared as she stomped down the beach in search of their leader.

Not Jackson, Melissa thought. *No need to bother him with a wardrobe malfunction.* She wanted Jackson to think of her as being calm and competent, someone he could count on in an emergency. She didn't want to look like a troublemaker. Like Taylor or Eric.

"I'm sorry!" Melissa claimed as she chased Taylor down the beach. "I don't know what else to say."

"Sorry?" Taylor waved the offending green shirt at her but never slowed down in her march toward Jackson. "That doesn't come close to covering it."

Melissa stumbled in some deep sand as she tried to catch up with Taylor. How had this girl lost so badly in Lex's maze race? Taylor could move fast when she wanted to. In the distance, Jackson was building something with rocks in a pit, and Melissa began to panic.

"Do we have to bother Jackson?" she asked.

Taylor held up the shirt like a bloody trophy from battle. "This was a gift from my daddy. Do you know how much it cost?"

"No," Melissa admitted, biting her lip.

"Well, neither do I," Taylor said with a frown, "but I'm sure it was more than your entire pathetic wardrobe!"

"Please don't make a big thing out of it."

"I'm just getting started." Taylor set her jaw and made straight for Jackson, who finally looked up from his mysterious labor.

Instantly, Taylor was all sweetness and light as she flirted with him. "Jackson, hi. I've got a teensy problem. It seems

Melissa here borrowed my favorite top without permission, and then—"

"I put it on by mistake," Melissa cut in. "It was dark. But then I got a smudge on it and I knew Taylor would freak, so I washed it and tried to dry it fast over the fire and—"

Taylor held up the shirt to show the results. *Only the tails are burned,* Melissa thought, *the rest of it is still usable . . . on a deserted island.* After all, it was a mistake.

"Ruined," moaned Taylor. "It's not like I have an endless supply of clothes here, like at home."

Both girls stared at Jackson, who sighed with exasperation. "So what do you want me to do?"

Taylor scowled and said, "Punish her."

"What?" Jackson asked. Melissa just stared in shock at the petite blond girl.

"Melissa should do all my chores from now on," Taylor said, "and give me the choice of any *three* of her shirts."

"Three?" Melissa complained. "I've only got four!"

Taylor crossed her arms and looked unsympathetic. "It's about value, not quantity."

Melissa shook her head and tried to keep her mouth shut, because arguing with Taylor was pointless. So was stooping to her level of outrage.

To Melissa's relief, Jackson said, "Lighten up, it was an accident." He turned to Melissa and added, "Just be more careful."

"No problem. Never again," she agreed. Melissa gave Taylor a conciliatory smile and hoped this would be the end of it.

"Problem solved," Jackson said, wiping the sand off his hands.

But Taylor was not satisfied, and her stare bored into Jackson, then shifted back to Melissa. "This isn't over," she declared through clenched teeth. She swiveled on her heel and marched away, clutching the singed top in her fist.

Melissa sighed, because she believed it when Taylor made threats. *I'll have to figure out some kind of peace offering.* She smiled sheepishly at Jackson, sorry for getting him mixed up in her mess-up. Though it was really Taylor who had dragged him in.

The big guy just went back to work, piling his rocks and ignoring her. Quietly, Melissa slipped away.